EVERY MAN'S HAND

Contents

In the Beginning

One sound, above all others, shrieked through the chaotic uproar of the battlefield. Just one stark sound, drilling into his mind. In a fraction of a second which seemed interminable, his brain concentrated itself on the whine of one approaching shell. Through the million other noises, it bored its way into his head and he knew, for certain, that this was the one which had been destined for him alone.

The smoke, the stench, the screams, the fear, the pain, were all just a backcloth to the lethal screech of the approaching missile. He hurled himself despairingly down to seek shelter in the stinking mud and he felt the blast and heard the explosion and cartwheeled through the air, landing deep in a water-filled crater, splashing, and spitting the mucky, oil-tasting liquid clear from his mouth and throat. Shaking, convulsively, with fear, he clawed his way to the shallow rim of the crater, collapsing, gasping at its edge and realising, with an immense relief, that he had survived, yet again. He became aware of a body beside him and turned to peer at it through the darkness. Suddenly illuminated, in the glare of an explosion, he saw it to be a headless corpse with one arm torn away. One of his comrades, who had lived, and now died, alongside him. In the obscenity of violent death, it had lost identity and he watched, horrified, as it slipped slowly into the green-brown slime of the crater, leaving a bubbling, crimson stain spreading in its wake. Tom knew the nauseous, bitter taste of vomit rising from his stomach to his throat and his body contorted with the violence of his retching.

He sat up, staring, sweating, shaking.

He always awoke at this point.

It was always the same.

He was just about used to it.

In the early months he had found it difficult to cope and fought off sleep, but now, after all these years, he could slump back into the pillows and breath deeply and slowly until he regained his composure. Then he would sit near to the bedroom window and spend time looking out over the fields. It always calmed him and he had often witnessed day come to the land and had sat, alone with his thoughts and memories, through nights of summer calm and winter spite. Sometimes he would wrap a blanket about himself and eventually doze off, waking stiff and sore from the wooden armchair.

He had survived the war and had learned to survive the peace.

The dream came less often and sometimes months would pass before his rest would be disturbed by it but he, or rather, his subconscious, would never again be freed from the terror of those cold trenches and putrid battlefields. The medals he now kept hidden away would never begin to compensate for those terrible years, when he, alone of his battalion that had started out, returned to civilian life, physically unscathed.

Why me?

He asked himself the question many times but could never find an adequate answer to it. He had been part of the greatest conflict ever known to man and had become indifferent to the carnage, never expecting to live to the next day, but he had come through it all. There are no unbelievers as the battle unfolds. Every living soldier places his trust and belief in the superior power of their God and hopes for special protection, even if, for many, He existed only in the form of the daily issue of the thick, mind-numbing, rum ration. His God had taken him under His wing right enough. Tom Thomas, or, as he would be known for the rest of his life, Tom Flanders, after the soul destroying region in which he had won his medals.

Anyone would have thought he had fought enough for one lifetime, and even *he* had been unaware of the bruising battles which would claim him in the immediate years of peace. Now it was 1933 and he hoped for a steadier, more tranquil existence.

Chapter 1

A Time to be Born

The warm, August night, had passed calmly and quietly, but dawn came with a chill to the oak-beamed cottage, curtained tightly at the windows to shut out the moonlight and shut in the bedroom blackness, and Tom Flanders had slept soundly, undisturbed by the labours of the black bitch. He had not been troubled with his nightmares that summer.

She lay still, almost motionless, on her side, in the deep wooden box which had once seen service as the bottom drawer in a long discarded wardrobe at the mansion. Safe in the sturdy compartment, she rested her head and occasionally flicked her tongue over her gleaming, damp puppies.

Grey dawn brought the surrounding hills to daytime as the darkness, almost reluctantly, loosed its grip, and the shadows slowly disappeared from the rooms as the first, early light poked fat fingers, tentatively, through the tiny, dusty windows, The black bitch was exhausted, but well content, and she lay peaceably with her four little whelps, now sucking at her strongly and shining like silken black seals. It was her second litter, and the births had been relatively easy and uncomplicated and she enjoyed her motherhood, prodding her muzzle at the whelps and cleaning them lovingly and dutifully with her moist tongue. She would be kind and caring and would be totally dominated by the needs of her little family for the next few weeks.

She was sensible and protective and a good mother.

She was a working terrier and earned her living, and her place in the kennel.

Her manner and appearance told plainly of her trade and though she was only four years of age, she had already worked three full seasons. Three seasons packed with effort and anguish and pleasure and pain and satisfaction for a job well done, as part of Tom Flander's team of terriers. Her ears were frayed and part of the left was missing, shorter now than the other, lost to a strong boar badger in the huge earth behind the old mansion. She has bled profusely for a time for ear wounds always appeared to be more serious than they actually were, but it had soon healed, and it caused her little discomfort, leaving merely a slightly lop-sided appearance. Her muzzle was scarred and her snout had been peppered from her many encounters with her main enemy, the fox, and her tongue had been split during the epic dig to a dog fox and his bride in the stony earth of Carreg. It had taken Tom five hours to reach her that stormy day and he had been alone for the last hour, digging through clinging clay, slithering and sliding in total silence, fearing the worst, but, when he eventually reached her, the bitch had killed them both and lay trapped, guarding her victims until Tom lifted her out, exhausted.

She was a working terrier and she was good at her trade.

She enjoyed the rough and tumble and ignored the slight discomfort of her occasional wounds. Curled up in the clean dry straw of her kennel, she would sleep away her aches and pains and wake refreshed with muscles cramped and stiffened, stretching and waiting for her walk to restore the suppleness to her body. Oh yes, her job was the control and destruction of the fox and yes, you could safely say she was good at it.

Though she would not be aware of it, she had, that summer night, given life to an animal that would surpass even her own considerable abilities. Laying close to her side and punching his paws about, the innocent scrap, that was to grown into a legend, began his life.

The small house came slowly alive, appearing spare and frugal without the homely glow of its fire, and Tom busied himself at the grate, setting the paper and sticks to draw fiercely and placing the largest cokes carefully to the burning wood until he was satisfied with its progress. He set some coals in position and, pleased with the now steady flames, he moved the large, black, iron kettle into its place to gather warmth, and spread his shirt and singlet over the fender.

Out now, into the little room where he kept his water, stored in buckets which he filled at the spring. He quickly washed himself, gasping at the shock of the cold water against his face and bare chest and flinching slightly as his skin tightened to the sting of his early morning ritual. Towelling himself briskly, he gathered his clothes from their place at the fire and dressed himself in front of the flames, enjoying the warmth and the reflections that danced around the room from countless brass and copper objects, giving the sparse area a new, and inviting, appearance. He opened the curtains and looked out over the fields, never failing to appreciate the scene before him and pausing to note a small ewe that hobbled slowly across his line of vision. He would need to check her feet later and would do so when he took the terriers for their early walk.

Satisfied with the appearance of the sky and knowing that the day would be bright and clear, he moved through the door to the adjoining room, where he had installed the mother-to-be in her clean whelping box two nights before. He peered in at the bitch who greeted him with a barely discernable tail wag, the slightest of movements, but a greeting all the same, and her own acknowledgement of her master's presence. She lay, proudly now, still stretched comfortably in her box, and waited as Tom, smiling slightly, spoke to her quietly, words of praise for her night's efforts.

Stroking her gently, he checked each whelp, noting their strong, healthy appearance, well pleased with the mother's sensible manner. Returning to his kitchen he prepared a dish of small-chopped rabbit, with a little milk, a light snack to reward the mother for she had earned it and would welcome it after her night's effort. She would need all her strength to rear the litter in style and Tom would see that she was well nourished. He placed the dish beside her in the box and she ate it greedily, raising only her head and not even moving from her prone position, but he had to disturb her, and so he shut her out in the garden while he cleaned and dried the box, removing the soiled bedding and laying down fresh, soft, barley straw. He checked the pups once again, more carefully. There were two bitches, level in size and coal black, but it was the smaller of the dogs pups which particularly impressed him. He was the only whelp with any white on the coat, a small blaze on the chest. Tom cupped him in his hands and noted, with satisfaction, that though he was only hours old, he was compact and sturdy and almost as tough as a badger cub, squirming in his palms and gaping as a finger touched the searching mouth, checking the gums and the palette and the wide, curved tongue.

The bitch was waiting anxiously and, as he let her back into the room, she lost no time in settling herself down and organising her family once more, not satisfied until she had nosed and licked each individual into the moist warmth of her teats.

Three days after their birth, Tom Flanders again shut the bitch out of the room. It was time to dock the tails of the whelps. For this purpose he kept a small scissors, with rather blunt blades, knowing from experience that their crushing effect would cause less blood loss than the use of a sharp, clean-cutting edge. He measured the length carefully for it was a crucial moment that could mar the terrier's appearance. Too short a cut would result in a stump like appendage with hardly anything to grip on when the dog needed to be removed from the earth, and too generous a length left on would tend to curl the tail over the terrier's back, almost like a sail. It was an easy matter to shorten the tail once he had decided on the correct length, and the pups hardly noticed the small operation. A slight squeak, and application of the balm used to staunch the insignificant blood loss, and the whelps were once more nestled into the warmth and care of their dam.

The mother and her family had missed the easy spring and lazy summer which would have helped to build their constitution but now, enjoying their nearness, the bitch stretched and yawned and gave her immediate life to her sons and

Growing into independent and confident terriers

daughters. For the next few weeks her attention was focused on her maternal duties and her world consisted of the confines of her whelping box, which Tom had moved back out to the kennels after the first, crucial days had passed. He took great care to keep the other terriers away from the pups' quarters and if any, with curiosity, strayed even to the rough, dry-stone wall surrounding them, the bitch would be immediately on her guard, rushing out, prepared to deal with any emergency and ready to see off unwelcome intruders.

During the third week she became less possessive and would allow the pups to explore, on their still unsteady legs, darting about in small, quick, charges and losing balance at any unevenness in the floor, or strange object in their path. Their squeaks and squawks slowly changed to purring growls as, in their puppy challenges, they stood menacingly before each other, and the increasing activity of their life contributed to their steady growth. They were now taking sloppy, but solid, food and becoming less dependent on their mother, who was glad to be free of them. How quickly the joys of motherhood had changed to boredom, and possessiveness to indifference. She wearied of their clamour, and so they found themselves progressively left to their own devices, thriving and growing and developing into independent and confident terriers.

Tom had watched them carefully as the weeks passed and spent many an hour keeping observation as they scuttled about, daily venturing further from the kennel until their horizons knew no boundaries, following each other over the fields and through the hedges and standing in wonder and awe before the large, imperturbable sheep. The small dog pup had once faced up to the burly ram, mere inches from each others face, standing immovable for minutes, as if hypnotised. Tom had watched with interest, from a distance and was pleased to see the incident end when the ram, becoming bored, butted the youngster contemptuously into the ground, stamping at him for good measure. The pup had made no sound, but had backed away slowly and carefully, before quickly retreating with as much dignity as he could muster, glancing behind occasionally at his giant aggressor, doubtlessly pleased that no pursuit had been made. For the rest of his life he would respect these dull, but solid animals, and would remain steady, even when caught up, alone, in the middle of an unruly and frightened flock, with lambs leaping and springing all about him.

When they were twelve weeks old, Tom parted with the rest of the litter and sent them off to their new homes, where he could reclaim them should the need ever arise. The little dog was already something of a character and showed no sign of missing his companions, for he was quite at ease in the company of the older terriers. His owner considered naming him for the mark on his chest but decided that "Blaze" would be better suited to a pony than a working terrier. No, he would beep it simple and unpretentious. He would not burden him with anything fancy, for the pup itself appeared to be stolid and dependable rather than flambouyant. He was, however, a distinctive dog and deserved a name to match. He thought back to his own short career.

He decided to call him Bruiser.

Puppy days passed quickly that winter and spring and when his first summer came to an end as the leaves left the trees and the first frosts lightly gripped the fields, Bruiser had thrown off his immaturity and adopted the attitude of his comrades from the kennels. It was as if he had never been a pup. True, in his early months, he would tear papers apart and shake at the sweeping brush with fury. He would pull at socks and trouser legs, but he did it with a deadly earnest manner and had no playful intentions. He would scuffle with his mother, but even then, his attitude would be serious and the games would often end with the bitch breaking off the encounter. At thirteen weeks, while skulking about the yard, he had found a large rat, caught live in a cage trap, and though it was his first sight of a rodent, his fury was such that he destroyed the cage, wrenching the unfortunate creature through the twisted bars, disregarding the dirty, yellow-brown teeth, and killing it quickly, shaking it as if it were a toy, until he discarded the lifeless, shapeless mess. He would sometimes worry away at one of his kennelmates, riling them to severe retaliation but the pup, instead of showing abject fear, or submission, by rolling on his back as he should, would warily stand his ground, turning his head slightly aside, appearing to be prepared to take his punishment, rather than show remorse.

He had character, and through that first winter, he had enjoyed his exercise walk with his elders, never lagging behind, splashing across marsh and icy streams and forcing his way enthusiastically through, over or around the most daunting obstacles. He never appeared to tire and he would be among the first to check every small drain or patch of bracken or gorse. No cover could deter him and he would force his racy shoulders into the most narrow of entrance holes in partly-closed earths or buries. As his first spring came to the land he had already shed his milk teeth and though he could not yet know what he was seeking, occasionally his nostrils would twitch to the whiff of a tantalising scent that stirred some primitive force deep within him. His body would tense and the hairs on his neck and back would stiffen.

He was destined to follow that scent all his days and seek out its source in dark passages, deep in the earth. It would become the very reason for his existence, totally dominating his life like some powerful, addictive drug and calling to him with a message which he could never ignore.

Chapter 2

Under the Oaks

Heavy with cub, her body low to the ground, she moved slowly past the meadow. Skirting the field cautiously, keeping close to the shelter of the blackthorn hedge and scarcely visible, she often disappeared completely from sight as she dropped into the shallow ditch.

Though the rain was now persistent and heavy, the ditch, shielded by the hedge, was still dry and the vixen, using its shelter, managed to avoid the worst of the weather until she had almost reached he destination.

She was very near to her time now, and, with some relief, she slipped cautiously into the secluded, small, rocky earth in the oak-covered slope where she had spent the recent nights scratching the loose soil earnestly and frantically until it was to her liking. Withdrawing to the furthest extremity of the tunnel, she knew her cubs would be born very soon and when next the sun appeared, to a bright, clean day, she nursed four small whelps snugly to her teats.

She had been without her partner for the past fourteen nights and knew that the litter, never to see their father, would depend for their survival on her efforts alone. It would be more difficult than last year when the dog fox had assisted her, often bringing a rabbit or fat fowl to help feed her and raise the hungry brood through their early weeks. He had been struck by a lorry which lumbered along the seldom-used road one early morning, flinging his handsome tawny body to the grass verge and going on its way without pause, snarling and rumbling by in a cloud of dust and exhaust fumes. She had only narrowly avoided contact herself and, frightened, paused but briefly to nose and nuzzle the crimson-soiled form of her dead made.

It was the way of the wild and she would have to cope.

Time passed easily as she suckled the blind cubs. She had been able to build up her strength in the end-of-winter months, for the climate had been kind after the early frosts. January and February had been exceptionally mild and though March brought some light, snow flurries, it had quickly cleared and the land had come to spring without knowing the usually relentless grip of icy winter. She had fed well and had seldom been in such fine, fit condition for motherhood. She had hunted and scavenged with great success and was fairly bursting with health. Her thick coat glistened and her ears, like dark velvet patches, gleamed in witness to her well being. The litter would be but a small problem to her, once the critical early weeks had passed.

During the three years of her life she had known little anxiety though she lived with the typical, restless caution of her kind. In her remote country she encountered man infrequently and had found him to be of more assistance than threat, though her instincts told her of his hostility. Sometimes a questing cur dog made her step lively, but such meetings were only a minor disturbance and caused her little alarm. Man, and his dogs, had so far been easily outwitted or outrun and had actually provided for her, as she made good use of his fields and shelters and discarded rubbish. She had prepared well for her confinement and her milk was abundant. The cubs thrived and when their sticky eyes eventually opened to the bleary near-darkness of their home, they were, like all young things, a splendid sight. As yet lacking the distinctive "foxy" appearance, they were dark brown in colour with blunt muzzles yet to develop the typical, sharp features which would come later, as they grew.

Their days and nights were spent in sleep, awakening only to tax their dam with demands for her food and warmth. She was a good provider and, as their sharp spiky teeth appeared and their appetites improved, she would leave their hiding place, returning when she was able to carry with her something for the eager, hungry brood. Her re-appearance was always keenly anticipated for the cubs were ever impatient at their feed time.

Days and weeks passed quickly in their close world, and as their strength increased and they grew in size, they became ever more demanding of their mother's labours and even more adventurous in their movements, restlessly attempting to make their way to the entrance of their private world.

After darkness had descended over the fields, the cubs would be allowed to leave their shelter and in the freedom of the fresh air and the cool breezes, their release would be frenzied. Leaping and pouncing, and chasing playfully, they would soon exercise any stiffness from their limbs in the exhilaration of glorious escape from the cramped confines of their stuffy underground home. Never had wild things so enjoyed their games and at times, their mother, though ever watchful and suspicious, would join with them, using the pastime to help provide the stealth and awareness so essential for their future lives. They would stalk each other through bracken and heather, always ending with a rush and a pounce and a scuffle of rolling fur, but however hard they tried, they were never able to surprise their mother for she would easily avoid their final plunges, no matter how warily they stalked her, and though joining in their games with an apparent careless manner, she was never found to be off her guard. The cubs must develop the very same qualities.

She transmitted her nervous demeanour to her family and the least extraordinary sound or scent would send them all scuttling to the safety of their earth. A tawny owl, often watching, sphinx-like from his perch in the oaks had seen such antics before but still found it all a puzzle. The cubs were unaware of the reason for this excessive caution and yet, through their play, and by their mother's example, the typical reactions of their kind were being implanted for life. Never a day would pass when they would be free from their readiness to react to danger. They would survive by absorbing these lessons and refining the instincts for caution which were being imparted to them at such an early age.

Their home became increasingly foul.

The vixen had little difficulty in her search for food and the atmosphere became ever more foetid with the stench of rotting meat, little scraps left, half eaten. She had, unwittingly, chosen their first home on the land of a man of increasing age and failing health and, at lambing time, the carcass of both fallen ewe and lamb, lay all about her. It was a simple matter to keep her brood well fed though this carrion would never be their favourite meal, and, in the midst of such abundance, much was wasted, or hidden, to rot and stink below the ground and around the entrance to their den. Green flies swarmed angrily at the warren and the stench was now noticeable at some distance, and this brought the youngsters their first experience of the terror that lay in wait in the life before them.

The mother would leave the earth for long periods during daytime and the cubs, though as yet too cautious to venture outside the entrance in her absence, found the temptation increasingly difficult to resist. They would approach the mouth of the tunnel, jostling each other impatiently, as the warm air with its fresh scents of early summer reached them, but, lacking confidence, not one was ready for a daylight exploration. They had become accustomed to the sounds which reached their ears and the calls of the lapwing and curlew from the meadows were familiar to them. Sheep grazed nearby and scavenging crows and magpies shouted their raucous, mocking calls. Once a hedgehog had moved ponderously by, peering inquisitively into their home with short-sighted eyes and causing the nervous cubs to stare in amazement, before hastily withdrawing, scurrying away, pushing into each other, into the safety of the darkness. They had never before seen such a creature, but now the scent from their bury brought them a more sinister visitor.

The cubs were close to the mouth of the tunnel, confident and sure that before many more days passed, one of their number would take the first tenuous steps into the sunshine. They lay still, facing the fresh air current, nostrils twitching, analysing every scent, drowsily waiting the return of their mother. She would appear, silently as a shadow, blotting out the light as she forced her way into the earth, always causing the cubs to react with surprise.

Now sudden darkness came with the most awful roar and frightening scent. Heavy jaws snapped and hot, fierce breath filled the little lungs. Petrified for an instant, they surged, in panic, to the depths of their tunnels, pushing tightly and burying their heads into each other for refuge. Three cubs, cowering as the screams of their sister mingled with the furious roars of her persecutor. Mercifully, her agony was quickly over and her lifeless body was shaken, limply, in the jaws of the monster.

For so he appeared to the small, smitten family.

He could be heard plainly, growling and snarling and digging with fury in an attempt to reach the remaining cubs. The broken body of his victim lay on the grass, her first appearance outside her home in daylight. The monster worked with a feverish anger, ripping at roots, denied the chance for further victims, for the cubs were well out of his reach and their tormentor was unable to force his bulky shoulders any further into their home. For more than an hour he tore and scratched at the earth, making no progress, until at last, he tired and his efforts grew less and an uneasy quiet came upon the place that had been their safe home.

The collie, for such was the monster, had broken off his efforts and was now almost back at his master's cart. The farmer was well used to the appearance of his dog in such a dishevelled state, covered in earth and spattered with blood, for he had ended the life of many a fox, often digging deep into badger setts and once having become firmly stuck. It had taken almost two hours to dig him out with the help of a neighbour.

Only the demands of the lambing season had caused their visit to the area. The farmer smiled. It had been a worthwhile trip and he was well pleased with the animal for few sheepdogs took so readily to the pursuit of the fox. The dog was an asset in every way. Calling the collie beside him, he took up the reins and they began their bumpy way home, the cart lurching violently along the rough, rutted tracks. They had some distance to go and though their path crossed that of the vixen, they were not aware of her presence.

Guided and urged on by some intuitive foreboding, she became careless in her haste and concealment was not her first priority. She cursed the bold magpies which accompanied her. Flying low about her, they mocked her with their cries, delighting in her discomfort and rejoicing at the sorry sight which met her at the end of her journey. Already carrion crows had pecked at the head of her smallest cub, and with a dreadful haste, she entered the warren. Never had the young foxes greeted their mother with such relief! They pressed to her and she gathered them about her in the familiar, protective manner. Still they shook with the memory of their terror, while the vixen, in grief at the loss of one, licked and smoothed the three with her gentle tongue.

She resolved to move her family that night to a fastness as far away from their birthplace as they could possibly travel.

The encounter with the sheepdog reinforced the cub's awareness of the need for caution in their lives. The sudden transformation of a drowsy afternoon by such an event would serve to remind them just how precarious was existence in the wild, natural world, and the helpless cries of their sister instilled in them a bitter lesson which they would not forget.

The vixen had become more nervous than ever, and she had to summon every reserve of courage even to leave their home that night, but as darkness came to end the day, her muzzle slowly appeared at the entrance and she tested the air warily, for long moments, her nostrils twitching nervously, before venturing forth, and even then she hesitated, but eventually called to her cubs to follow.

In the pallid moonlight, the old oaks with wrinkled trunks and branches all twisted into painful-looking, arthritic postures, took on a cruel, menacing air, and she did not look at the crumpled form, so hideous in death after the attention of the carrion eaters. In such a mood of gloom and caution did the depleted family begin their journey, leaving behind their first happy home.

Silently, in single file, they padded along behind their mother in a subdued exodus. The usually wicked and boisterous dog fox brought up the rear, close behind his two remaining sisters, and never once did he playfully seize their small tails of nip at their heels. The serious business of living had begun for them all and they would practice frivolity at their peril, and so she led them to their new life, her urgency communicating itself to each member of her family.

Grief, in the wilderness, is a fleeting thing and cannot be sustained. It is nature's way, and the vixen threw off her mantle of sorrow and once more lent herself to the task at hand. The education of her litter, for life's journey, must now be resumed in earnest.

The night sky was cloudless and, using the moonlit shadows, the little procession made good progress. The vixen stopped many times to test the air and occasionally she would come to a halt in mid-stride, standing motionless until the cause of her caution had been recognised. Behind her, the cubs mimicked her ever move and gesture and presented a pretty sight, had there been any prying eyes.

Crossing the lane by the old badger path, they were quickly through a hedge and into an extensive gorse-covered bank, gaining some shelter from the keen wind which swept along behind them. Skirting a farmyard with caution, they carried on with no sign of tiredness or complaint from the youngsters and though they had been moving for some hours, the vixen still showed no sign of easing the pace until, at last, they stopped above a huge chasm. It looked, to the cubs, as if the world had suddenly come to an end. Motioning the young foxes to wait, the vixen moved dexterously down the steep rock face, following a narrow sheep track, no more than a ledge, until she disappeared from sight into the cavernous belly of the quarry.

She had not been gone long before the young dog fox peered anxiously over the rim of the rock, but his eyes could see no bottom to the darkness and anxiety came again to the young cubs. It was most unusual for the vixen to leave them stranded when out hunting and they were unable to understand this new course of events.

He moved towards the sheeptrack.

He would follow her and find the reason for her absence.

Even as he took his first steps along the path, his mother's form loomed suddenly out of the darkness and, warning her family to take care, she led them down the steeply sloping cliff. As they rounded the rock face, they travelled along grassy ledges made slippery with moss and dew and they passed the site of an old peregrine falcon nursery where white bleached bones and fading feathers marked the shelf where young birds had once stood patiently, waiting for the gift of flight to come to their wings. Slender young silver birch trees clung to flimsy footholds, bent like bows before the winds and as the cubs continued their slow descent, rabbits could be seen moving with sure footed speed along the ledges, sending showers of small stones tumbling into the void below. At last they reached their new home. The vixen had chosen well.

A broad patch of level, stunted grass, gave way to a narrow entrance into the rock and as they pushed their way through the tight aperture they could see tunnels leading in many directions. The stench of rabbit was very strong and the rocky corridors were barely wide enough to pass through in some parts.

They would be safe here.

Leaving the cubs, she made her way out into what remained of the night. There was still time to provide a meal for them all before the day emerged from the darkness. The cubs, in their new home, closed into a tight huddle and were soon asleep, for they had travelled far that night and, though hungry, were very tired.

Unknown to them, or to their mother, they had entered the country of the Garth Valley Foxhounds.

Chapter 3

Tom Flanders

The weary wind from the morning woke, fresh from its afternoon slumbers and raced, with a re-born urgency through the early evening. Crashing among the mountains and dancing violently along the quarry face it plucked at the birch saplings as if seeking to tear them from their roots. The icy fingers searched among the crannies but the cubs took no heed, safe in their deep snugness.

On, down to the hamlet, to torment the chimneys, hurling the smoke back into their throats and choking cottagers huddled together in their inglenooks. Through the village and past the chapel and the pub, on now to the spinney by the river, testing doors and windows for every crack and forcing a freezing entry into the warm kitchen. The small cottage crouched for shelter among the trees and Tom Flanders poked firmly at the firegrate, lifting the coals and placing a bulky holly log on the top. The flames burned brightly and leapt to the darkness of the chimney and Bruiser, stretched out on the floor before the heat, yawned, fit to crack his jaw.

What a life for a working terrier!

Tom Flanders was testing his new theory, and Bruiser was his experiment. He would let this terrier live in his home. He would take him with him, wherever he went and he would expose him to every possible situation. There were those that said a worker belonged in the disciplined surrounds of the kennel, but Tom was prepared to try out his new conviction. He hoped the dog would gain intelligence without becoming mollycoddled and spoiled and though his other terriers were kennelled, Bruiser shared his master's hearth and his master's life.

What more could a worker want?

As spring came to the land he had already shed his milk teeth and though Tom never allowed him to sleep on the bed, he rested on the floor, at the foot of it, each night. Throughout the first year of his life he was rarely more than ten feet away from his master, for the young terrier and the quiet, dour man were two of a kind, happy in each others' company and content with their life.

As a boy, Tom had led a secluded country existence, remote but never lonely, though he was an only son. His sister was much younger and had no interest in Tom's ferrets and wild animals, tamed and tended, nursed and cured of illness or injury. He was as one with the countryside and loved its solitude. He hated school. He hated his teacher. "Come outside Thomas Thomas, spell 'righteous' on the blackboard for us, if you please." The brightest children in the classroom would giggle and laugh and poke fun, for he could barely write his name. "Don't be shy Thomas Thomas. Are you shy or are you stupid?"

He hated school.

He hated his teacher.

He was at his best in the fields, in the forests, roaming the mountains. He was at ease in the wind and the rain, in frost and storm. He was never shy with his animals.

When he was just twelve, his mother had died and this great sadness in his life meant that his unpromising academic career came to an abrupt end. He found work as a farm servant, hard work and long hours, but work which he enjoyed, and the food was good and there was enough of it. His employers were kindly people and treated him as part of their own family and, whenever he was able, he even helped out at home, for his father found it difficult to cope with the requirements of a young daughter. She needed a mother, and before a year had passed she had one, a pleasant enough woman from the village, but Tom never accepted her. He only acknowledged one mother and she was gone. This new woman was just another wife for his father, someone else for Tom to resent, and before General Kitchener even pointed his finger at the nation, Tom was gone, to join the great adventure of war against the Hun. He left no note, no explanation. He confided in no one, but they knew he would not be back. He had given away his two terriers and his ferrets and loosed his small menagerie back into the wild. It took him two days to walk to the army barracks, only to be turned away when he correctly gave his age as sixteen. "Come back tomorrow" said the sergeant, "When you are eighteen", and so he was issued with his first uniform.

He was big and strong and silent and painfully aware of his faltering English, for he had spoken only Welsh for most of his life and used English only sparingly, at school or whenever he had no alternative. He thought in Welsh and sometimes he would have to pause, groping in his mind for the correct English word and often he would not know that word. It gave his comrades the impression that he was dull. A stupid country boy. It led him into barrack room conflicts which he did not know how to avoid and it loosed in him powers that he had not known he possessed. Soon his fellow infantrymen became wise enough to leave him well alone and, after his first year, in a camp near London, he spent the rest of the war fighting the enemy. Until his arrival at the hell of Passchendaele, he had enjoyed army life. He had accepted the discipline and relished the hard physical grind of training. Fitness was a priority and the newly formed Physical Training section, raised to whip soft civilians into toughened soldiers, drew many of its instructors from the professional boxers of the time. The troops were expected, even ordered, to take part in the ring sport and it was during this period that Tom experienced the loneliness and self reliance of the fist fighter.

He loved it.

The sport suited his solitary character.

He spent every off-duty moment in the gym, an eager pupil and a quick learner. He became middleweight champion of the regiment, knocking out his opponent, a young officer who had gained his boxing blue at Oxford. It opened new doors for Tom and when the great "Peerless" Jim Driscoll visited the battalion,

Tom was given the privilege of boxing three rounds with the master. He towered over Driscoll, outweighing him by almost two stone and making him look emaciated as they posed together for a photograph, but he never forgot the boxing lesson he was given that night in front of the assembled troops. He could scarcely lay an angry glove on the wonderful old ringman and the photograph taken that evening was treasured for the rest of his life. He was impressed, but so was Driscoll and in his sincere way, he invited the youngster to look him up at his Cardiff training quarters when the big bout with Germany finally ended. Tom was delighted with the invitation but it didn't pay to look that far ahead.

Over in France and Belgium, army life was another matter.

As men fell in the filth, never to rise again, as pals of the morning became the maimed of the evening, as vital, living flesh transformed into the rotting carcasses of no-man's land, his character cemented into the dour manner than only rarely left him throughout his later life.

He made no plans in readiness for war's end for he did not expect to survive that long. He saw new faces come to the lines and old faces leave, crippled physically and mentally as the senseless carnage continued. As wave after wave of doomed, damned, manhood fell before the guns and filthy clouds of gas, he saw men drown, wounded, in flooded craters and stepped on putrifying swollen bodies as he charged blindly at the enemy across the wasteland that separated them. His comrades fell like flies and he became more reckless. Why should he survive when so many good men perished? Every day that dawned over the slimy, rat-infested battlefield, was a day he never expected to survive, and he lived, almost in a daze, oblivious to the passing of time or the cruel discomforts of the front. And then, suddenly it seemed, it was all over. Incredibly, at the end of 1918, he found himself, with his kit bag on his shoulder, walking outside a railway station in a grim old mining valley as the train panted slowly away, winding between the mountains. He was not yet twenty-one years of age and it was time he took his place in the land fit for heroes.

He found work immediately, and though the daily drop into the earth's belly unsettled him, he soon accepted it. After the hell of war, he could overcome anything.

Within weeks he had a terrier of sorts and even managed to find a ferret though, he thought, there'll be little sport to be had in the teeming, tumultuous, smoke-filled industrial wastelands. He took lodge with a young mining widow and kept his terrier in the back garden, where he build a small kennel, and he began to carry his ferret to work in a stout canvas bag. The damp workings of the mine where he toiled, harboured more rats than colliers, and as soon as he had become accustomed to the wet, confined, cold passages, he set himself to their slaughter. He became too useful to prop roadways and soon he worked with the pit ponies in the underground stables, feeding them, tending their ills, training them to their unnatural life style and killing the rats which would eat as much corn as the horses it left unchecked.

He settled quickly into the routine of the little valley community and enjoyed the company and comradeship of his fellow miners. It was not unlike the army. The danger was still present, though on a lesser scale, but the trials of the trenches had prepared him well enough for the hardship of labour, deep below the earth's surface. All life paraded before him and the pit was a cross section of all that was good, and bad, in human nature. Devout, God-fearing men worked alongside foul-mouthed, ignorant beer swillers, and men who could recite poetry and spent their little spare time seeking eduction, rubbed coal-grimed shoulders with pugilists and hard men, with hard lifestyles. Underground, each relied upon the other for safety, and close involvement brought understanding and tolerance to the majority of the men. The pubs and music halls were well patronised, but so were the chapels and churches and many native Welshmen, perhaps only one generation removed from a country birthplace, still spoke effortlessly and easily in their native tongue. The younger colliers, in search of pleasure and with money to spend, frequented the billiard halls and theatres and played for, or followed, the local football teams. Most would have started work in the pit at fourteen years of age and would arrive quickly at an early manhood. Tom, returning from the Great War, had much to do to catch up with them. At his age, many had become skilled colliers and as he was new to the job, the menial, labourers' tasks were all that came his way. He did not complain, but when his gift for handling animals became evident he was transferred to the underground stables, working with the pit ponies. It was not an easy matter to introduce a horse to the life of toil. First he would have to be led through the colliery yard on his way to the cage which would drop him below ground and the hissing steam and clanking trucks and screeching hooters could be a terrific ordeal for an animal unused to such things. By the time they arrived at the cage, the horses could be capricious and sometimes decidedly dangerous. Tom always used patience and kindness and rarely resorted to violence unless under extreme circumstances, and to him fell the task of training many new pit ponies for the sentence of toil for the rest of their life. Most were four years old when they came to him and already set in their ways but, using his own methods, he would break them to their new life style quicker than any of the other men and, more often than not, turned out steady, dependable animals. His gift was invaluable. He knew his charges would leave the mine when they were no longer of any use, and the next time they saw the sun's rays, they would usually be on their way to the knacker's yard. It was not all that different for the men, he thought, for violent death or lingering, lung-racking illness was all that most could expect for their labours.

Pit ponies were essential to the operation of the mine and were well cared for and well treated by their handlers. Only men with good horse technique would be employed as ostlers or hauliers and dismissal was the inevitable result of ill treatment of their charges. The system of underground roadways was complicated and a good team of pony and ostler were a great asset.

At the pit head, one freezing day in January, he saw the foxhounds on the mountain breast. The great, shaggy-coated Welsh hounds sang their wild, mournful notes to the wind, in full cry as they ran their fox into an old drift mine air shaft. The fearless, melancholy music stirred a primitive passion within him and he watched, fascinated, as the riders drew up to the milling hounds, marking now at the narrow, overgrown, dilapidated entrance to the shaft.

Many of the valley notables were there, mounted on sturdy Welsh cobs and dressed almost informally, and not in the manner of the grand, fashionable hunts. The master stood out, a colliery owner, important, in charge, above the crowd.

"Whip them off huntsman. Leave him, Give him best. We'll send no terrier into that shaft."

It was wise. Who knew what poison lurked in the trapped, still air within its confines? How could a terrier face a silent, invisible foe which could kill him more efficiently than any fox or badger? The master liked to show off his hounds to his colliery employees, liked to believe they appreciated this small opportunity to share his sport. If only he knew! While some were keen, most would much have preferred an improvement in their living conditions and enough food for their families and to hell with him and his hounds.

Tom though, like many, earned a reasonable wage. Enough for his unpretentious needs for he neither smoked nor drank, and his animals, at work or in his own time, were his only concern.

Harnessing one of his ponies for the start of another shift, he passed it on to a new man, temporarily engaged as a haulier. He was a stranger to Tom who was not slow to take a dislike to the man. The hauliers had a genuine respect and affection for their horses. They were rough perhaps, but so were the times and the men who tended the horses cared for them as best they could as if in sympathy with them in the unnatural conditions man and horse were called to work in. He saw the new man ill-treat, what had been a good-natured pony, on many an occasion, and after one particularly brutal onslaught, Tom threw the man to the ground and would have fought him there and then had not a fireman quickly intervened, forcing his way between the grappling forms. Fighting underground was a serious offence. The matter must be settled after work.

The news soon circulated through the pit and the men's support was mostly for Tom, though they pitied him. Had he not realised that he had picked a quarrel with an ex-middleweight champion of Wales? A former professional boxer and an experienced booth fighter, "Bull" Baker knew it all. He could box and he could fight, clean or dirty. He had been in with the best and it was only his intemperate habits and inability to sustain rigorous training that had caused him to fall just short of the very top. Out of condition now, but even allowing for his beer-pot, he would still murder Tom in a rough-house mountain fight.

The youngster must go through with it and, when the two men squared up, surrounded by miners on the rough slopes above the pit, no one expected much of a contest but close observers might have thought differently. Stripped to the waist, in trousers and heavy pit boots, "Bull" Baker's paunch spoke silent volumes. His biceps were fleshy and his once well-formed pectoral muscles sagged. Tom had the shoulders of an ox and the iron-hard arms of a blacksmith. His neck grew square and strong from his solid frame and his torso tapered to a well muscled midriff. Had he stripped to his shorts, his legs would have appeared almost spindly, too thin to support his bulk. Like the classic middleweight he was later to become, the upper body was a storehouse of tremendous power and alone, facing his opponent, the familiar feeling of confidence came flooding to him.

No contest.

But it was the experienced "Bull" who was quickly pounded to defeat. Closing immediately, he had brought his knee into Tom's groin and attempted to butt with his great bony head but a heavy left soon had him reeling. The vicious, clinical hitting of the youngster sent blood snorting from the ex-champion's nose and the punch that would make Tom famous was seen in the valley for the first time. The devastating left hook to the body, clubbed the wind from "Bull's" dust-shrouded lungs and the following punch, another left which struck high on the temple, sent "Bull" crashing to the coaldust floor.

There were those present who knew raw talent when it appeared so obviously, and Tom soon spent most of his free time in the gym at the back of "The White Hart". He smashed his way through his early contests with such ease that his frightening left was soon reported as having felled a bull for a bet, striking the beast firmly on the forehead and poleaxing it to the ground. So was myth and legend formed from his pit-head brawl, and with training quarters for potential fortune seeking fighters at the back of almost every valley pub, he had no difficulty in finding opponents and often fought three times a week, sometimes conceding two stone, and felling, out-of-condition heavyweights.

His earnings increased but still he lodged with his widow woman, carefully saving his money, and even when, three years later, he fought Reuben Taylor in an eliminator for the British title, he needed a great deal of persuading to go into a proper training routine and take time off work.

Reuben could box. He was not a hard hitter but her threw so many fast, stinging punches that he stopped most of his opponents, cutting them or relentlessly sapping their spirit. He boxed behind a straight left in the traditional style and his face was still remarkably well preserved after a lifetime of pugilism. He had once held the title, but his best days were gone and his blinding speed had waned and Tom knocked him out in the fourth, piling his uncoordinated body to the canvas near the corner, where his seconds quickly stepped in to tend him, and steady his convulsing limbs.

It was only matter of time before his punching power and durability took him to London and the British title but he was never to fight for it. For some months he had found it difficult to "make a fist" and the condition deteriorated so rapidly that within six months his left hand could not be closed, and pain shot through his arm if he even lightly tapped the heavy training bag. Fending off punches from his sparring partners became painful, almost impossible, and when he landed his own blows, the self-inflicted agony in his hands, his arms, his shoulders, would be greater than that felt by his opponent.

His trainers coated his hands in warm wax cocoons, soaked them in brine, tried every means and method known in the world of the pugilist but it was no use.

His hands, his fighting weapons, could no longer blast out their lethal message. He was finished.

Arthritis, at his early age, had brought an end to a career that would have been legendary and could even have culminated in a world title battle against Harry Greb, the "human windmill". Tom's fighting life ended as suddenly as it had begun, but now he became even more withdrawn and morose.

He changed his jobs, never staying anywhere very long, and he changed his lodgings, leaving the steadying influence of his young landlady. He let himself go. He drifted and drank and began to waste his life. He had enjoyed the atmosphere of the ring. The lights, the crowds, the smoke, the smell.

The isolation.

Best of all, the isolation. How he had relished it. No matter how many spectators packed into the halls to see him, at the first bell, he was alone. Sitting on his stool between rounds, he was still alone. Seconds gave him water, moistened his dry mouth, someone spoke to him, advice, advice, vaseline smeared his face, cuts were tended, all in a trance-like haze that shut it all out.

He was alone.

He felt secure.

As the years passed, the story of the fighting ostler grew stale and his increasingly surly behaviour exhausted what goodwill remained towards him until he found it hard to hold a job, and he wandered aimlessly through his life, eventually retracing his steps and heading away from the industry that had broken him like so many who had gone before.

By the time he was thirty-five he was back in the country, with enough money from his savings to buy the dilapidated cottage in the spinney. His needs were few. He would survive in an environment he had grown up with and knew how to handle.

His hand became less painful when the grind of the endless training had been left behind and he realised that the mighty, jarring effect of his punch had much to do with his suffering. He mended well enough and was able to grasp objects again and even swing an axe, so at least, his disablement had not been permanent. His new surroundings helped him to put his life back on course and he took up where he had left off, so many years before, tending to his animals and breeding his terriers.

Bruiser was the final part of his rehabilitation programme.

The little dog was a year old now, jet black, apart from his small, white, chest blaze, standing just thirteen inches at the shoulder and weighing fifteen pounds. He was something of a rarity, for black terriers were not popular and Tom's home county was more used to the white Sealyham or curs and crosses loosely described as fox terriers or Jack Russells. Some would call Bruiser a Lakeland, others, unkind, or ignorant, a mongrel, and while it was true that his grandfather had been a dog from the Cumberland fells, Tom cared not for the opinions of others. He knew exactly how the dog was bread and as far as the was concerned, Bruiser was simply a working terrier. He was sensible, he was brave, he was strong, and he would, in his own working future, never give up. Bruiser was Tom, in canine form, for Bruiser was also a loner and knew only one master but he differed from Tom in one significant aspect.

Tom loved foxes. Even though he hunted them and would kill many in the years that lay ahead.

Bruiser hated foxes and would hate them all through his violent life.

As the wind swirled angrily outside, the terrier stretched again, and twitched, whickering in his sleep and enjoying the comfort of the hearth.

Chapter 4

The Quarry Face

The vixen, and her three remaining cubs, spent two idyllic months in their home on the quarry face.

Every evening, as dusk came, she would lead an orderly procession up the sheep track to the cliff top. They often saw the young peregrine near to the edge but he would launch himself into space before they approached too closely. He would plummet down, down, then swoop to a ledge, or rise to a prominent rock, rousing the parent birds to call noisily as they soared and glided above the foxes. Once the hen bird had appeared to attack the smallest vixen cub but her mother had seen the threat, which was all that it really was, and prepared to defend her. Peregrines preferred pigeons.

The quarry was a good home for the family group. They had grown accustomed to the scent of the men who worked at the stone and the cubs scavenged for discarded meal scraps when the shift was over and the quarry fell to silence after the day's activity. The young foxes were becoming adept at food gathering and were able to provide, sparingly, for themselves, without too much assistance from their mother. Rabbits, beetles, berries, worms, mice and voles had all become part of their diet and though they were surrounded by fields with sheep and well-grown lambs, the foxes never disturbed them.

Perhaps next year it would be different but now they fed only on fresh fallen carcass and found it tasty and entirely acceptable. The young dog fox developed into a most handsome cub. Already he was as big as his mother and far stronger than his sisters.

His sisters.

The smallest was always last to the meal, always ate whatever scraps were left after her brother and bigger sister had taken the best. No wonder she had been left behind, growing stunted almost, the weakest of the group. She would sit shivering on the quarry face as if even her coat was too meagre to keep out the chill evening air. It was as though she did not belong, but her mother still doted upon her, treating her even with favour over her more capable litter mates.

The day had been warm and, laying calmly on their ledge, they had caught the full warmth of the evening sun. They felt secure and sure of themselves and soon it would be time to start their nocturnal routine but now they lay basking lazily, grooming each other fitfully in the last heat of the day, waiting for the vixen's return. She had been away for some hours and often left them for prolonged periods.

They were still young and even though they were almost full grown and had been well taught, such an evening could easily cause their concentration to lapse. They sensed no danger until a shadow crossed their ledge and then, too late, the tainted scent reached their immature nostrils. In panic they sprang to their refuge but the bigger, stronger cubs were first, pushing the weaker vixen to the rear and the terrier was at her in a flash, tearing into her and throttling her quickly, ending her life in a matter of minutes as they struggled on the narrow ledge, mere inches from possible disaster for them both. He shook her about as her litter mates pushed further into the rocky lair, and then, dropping her still, warm body, he set off in pursuit.

Tom had last been aware of Bruiser, near to the cliff edge and now he was nowhere to be seen. He approached the chasm with care, to look over. He was never comfortable with heights and his head felt light and giddy but he forced himself to peer over, expecting to see the broken body far below. He had seen, instead, the black form hurrying down the sheep track and so he settled himself to wait for the terrier's return.

He must have chased after a rabbit.

He would be back soon.

Laying flat on his stomach, he looked down over the edge and, searching the rocks, he saw the young peregrine and became so engrossed that he failed to notice the approach of the vixen until she stood, not ten yards from him. She moved slowly away, plainly attempting to draw him from the spot and he immediately realised that his young terrier had *not* been chasing after rabbits.

Choosing his steps with extreme caution and keeping his body flat to the cliff face, he forced himself to follow the steep path. He felt as if some gigantic force strained to push him into the void and he clung grimly to every rock and tufted handhold, squatting and shuffling along until, never daring to look into the chasm, he arrived at the grassy ledge where, at last, he became less tense. The musky scent of fox was overwhelming and, peering into the aperture in the rock face, he heard his young terrier baying somewhere below. His eyes, becoming accustomed to the gloomy half light, settled on the body of the young vixen and he knew that Bruiser had started his working career. He had killed his first fox. Now Tom was faced with the problem of calling him out. He started to move the loose rocks, dropping them behind him over the ledge and listening for long moments until they crashed into fragments on the quarry floor below, and soon he could hear the dog quite clearly. He pulled himself along the ledge, half his body wedged into the rocks and suddenly, the startling scream of the vixen pierced his ears. She stood on the ledge, almost at his feet, her agitation giving her courage as she sought, desperately to take the danger away from her cubs. Again she screamed, a ghostly, screeching noise, but her nerve broke as Tom scuffed his boots, kicking a shower of stone toward her, and she skipped away nimbly to the path top, seeming to invite the man to follow.

He worked quickly. He knew it would soon be dark and he could not trust an ascent of the perilous path without visibility. He knew that he was near to Bruiser but one careless move could dislodge loose stone to crash down onto the dog. He would keep trying for a few more minutes. He moved a massive slab, straining every muscle, inching it gingerly to the side and then he thrust his arm into the space below. His outstretched, groping fingers touched his terrier's stiff pelt and, straining further, he gripped him firmly by the tail, slowly easing the struggling form to the opening and manouvering him through.

Bruiser was furious.

He had been unable to reach the two remaining clubs.

They had backed into a tight space and now he wanted to return to them. The struggling and writhing of the dog could cause difficulties as Tom returned to the top of the quarry, could cause him to lose his balance. What if the dog were to squirm from his grasp? He solved the problem by letting the terrier worry the dead cub and, so occupied, carried both, as quickly as he dared, to the safety above, where he put a collar on the dog and led him away.

It had never been Tom's policy to kill cubs and though they were almost adults, he was relieved that only one had perished. He was saddened but, in the mysterious manner of those who work terriers, he was also elated. A young dog had shown good finding ability and working attitude and had known that the cubs were there. He had scented them from the cliff top and his breeding and inherited instinct had taken over.

While Tom ate his supper and Bruiser sprawled by the fire, the strong fox scent still heavy on the warmth of his pelt, the vixen claimed her remaining cubs. They moved again, to another home, settling in the forest, a short mile away, sheltered by the dense undergrowth of thorn and bracken and resting on the pine carpeted earth. Now they were three. The mother and her two cubs.

Two strong, healthy cubs.

Two fine specimens of their race.

Two youngsters any fox-mother would be proud of.

They had been attentive and learned their lessons.

They could survive alone in the wild.

Soon they would have to.

Just one week later, the Garth Valley Foxhounds began their season. As dawn broke, the young hounds were let into the forest to take up their careers. Hounds were to be trained to hunt, following the example of their elders, cubs were to experience being hunted. A family of foxes which did not separate were a greater threat to the farmer and cubbing, as it was called, served many purposes. It guided young hounds along the path to their destiny, it brought the pack to fitness and it split up the foxes, scattering them forever, weeding out any weak cubs fortunate to have survived thus far.

The cubs had never heard a hunting horn before and neither had their mother, but they knew instinctively that they must run, must seek a refuge. They kept together for a while but soon the leading hounds were too close and the vixen, leaving her cubs, veered to the left, hoping to draw the pack to her. The cubs crossed a small stream and then the dog fox turned, thrusting through the tangle of the forest floor, alone, for the first time in his young life.

Ruby and Radnor, and Dana and Teifi boomed their thunderous cry and followed the heavier-scented line of the mother, taking most of the pack along with them. She ran for her life as her vixen daughter made for the top of a steep fern bank, soon finding the effort too demanding through the clinging brambles. A lone hound closed upon the cub but in her desperation she sprang high, avoiding his lunge and twisted into the bracken. Scurrying under the fern, she plunged headlong into a big badger sett and the young hound, inexperienced, searched in vain and wondered where his enemy had gone.

Mother vixen crossed the road and ran along the river bank. She was calmer now, in full control of her faculties and she had gained on the hounds though she could still plainly hear their clamour. Stopping, she listened intently and the sound of voices ahead of her turned her away from her intended course. Loud shouts gave away her position and soon the leading hounds were only a field away as she pushed herself under a fence, losing precious seconds when the hounds cleared it without hesitation, taking the obstacle in their stride. In full view, she had only her speed and agility to save her.

It was not enough.

Ruby, the old queen of the pack, ended the vixen's life without delay and Dana was also present at the kill. The inexperienced vixen, new to the fury of the chase, had found it too much for her, its intensity showing her to be unprepared.

The daughter, terrified, lay safely in the badger sett and would know what to expect when next the sound of the hunting horn pierced the coverts. The son was safe away. He was no longer a cub, maturing quickly though still only seven months old, and his adult life had begun in earnest. He covered a mile and a half before he rested in some alders. It was cool alongside the river and he remained there for most of the day observing moorhens and mallards and the silver rippling surface where fish fed. A heron rose from the tall reeds at the bank, cumbersome, ungainly, gaunt and ghostly-grey with the cold, chiselled-from-stone look of a pterodactyl, and the young fox watched the strange creature and waited and learned.

He did not know that his mother had perished though some instinct told him not to search for her, and he did not know where his sister lay. He did not care, for he was safe and independent. He had won his first skirmish with hounds and won it easily. He could not know that his mother had, by her action, eased his path and, though it had cost her life, she had ensured his own. His first fears had passed and in his arrogance and confidence he saw himself as superior to these new pressures and he felt no alarm. He curled himself up on a dry rush bed and dozed fitfully until the first stars showed in the darkening sky above him. He hunted carefully that night and spent the next few days exploring his new territory and enjoying his freedom and self reliance.

Chapter 5

Cadno

He had no identity.

He was just a fox.

His mother was gone from his young life and his father had died before the cub had been born.

He had no name, as his two-legged enemies had names.

He had no name as their warrior earth dogs had names.

He answered no call as their great hounds obeyed the horn or their huntsman's voice.

He answered to no one.

He was a creature of the wild and would live a hard life. He would bring death to many lesser creatures, for he was a fox.

Men, his personal devils, would try to take him with hound and terrier. They would use trap and snare and gun and poison and all manner of evil to overcome him, for they hated and feared his wildness and would not understand. They would look upon him with contempt and he, in turn, would despise them. But he would also fear them and dread their proximity and know that he must be ever alert. His kind had but a short life, ever vigilant, and must live by their wits and wisdom and die for any carelessness.

He would not die as his father had died.

He would not die as his mother died, or his little vixen sisters.

He would live, and live well.

The life of an outcast and an outlaw would be his, but he would thrive.

He would know the cry of the pack.

Terriers would seek him in his resting places in the earth but freedom was his, a freedom that man's obedient dogs, his cousins, would never know.

No collar could bind him and no bars contain him for he had no master.

His fear would help to protect him and make him select his path with caution. His life would not be easily surrendered.

He was a fox.

Kill him if you can.

He was still in the country of the Garth Valley Hunt.

Soon, he *would* have a name.

* * * * *

The storm was near and the dark, purple clouds were scurrying in, breaking up the oppressive evening and bringing rain, badly needed, to the parched land.

Sharp lightning stabbed its way to earth and heavy thunder boomed and rolled violently through the skies as the rain swept over the fields, huge drops buffeting into the leafy trees and turning dusty paths into little waterways. Small birds went early to their shelters and a late-summer night came abruptly to the land. Autumn had been long delayed and was overdue.

The dog fox sought shelter from the downpour but could not find it, even in the compacted tangle of the forest floor, and he cowered apprehensively as the heavens roared their anger. His russet, white-throated coat took on a sad, spiky appearance and his handsome brush became heavily waterlogged and bedraggled as he continued to search, with little success.

As suddenly as it had begun, the electric upheaval passed and the earth gave off a new, tangy-fresh scent, welcoming the night creatures from their resting places. The tawny owl cried her mysterious cry and was answered from the far field, and rabbits settled to the vital business of living, venturing out to feed, loping into the soaking meadow. The badger lumbered from his sett and scratched at his belly before beginning his trundling travels in search of food. He would eat well as worms and beetles and snails welcomed the new dampness.

The young fox had claimed his place in the wild world and his first weeks of solitude had passed quickly. Every day brought him fresh adventure and he had hardly missed his family. He had caught and killed careless rabbits, digging one from the earth in a warren, and he had chased after and missed many more, as he wandered through the bountiful woods, taking note of all that surrounded him.

He shook himself violently, spraying the rain from his dense coat and drying his brush with quick, flicking movements before setting off in search of a meal. The forest floor was kind to him that night and like the badger, he took advantage of the earthworm harvest which had been triggered by the rain. Bilberries and blackberries helped to fill him and he was fortunate enough to find a rabbit dead in a snare. He carried it away to eat at his leisure, settling himself at the edge of a bank of scrubland as dawn streaked its first, pink shards into the sky. Cautiously leaving the matted denseness of bramble and bracken, he noted the movement of rabbits feeding some distance ahead of him. They were aware of his presence and as one or two showed their anxiety, began a withdrawal in a tumble of white scuts, hurrying to the safety of their warren. He stood, relaxed, watching, and made no attempt to take a young straggler that passed close to him. He had no need of another victim and, well sated, he watched it return to its refuge.

The morning was cool and clear, fresh washed from the heavy rain, as the country awoke to its new day. The fox lay concealed, lazily grooming, tired from his wanderings and ready to rest. He thought he might stay in these parts for food was plentiful and, after renewing his energy with rest, he would make himself even more familiar with his territory.

At the kennels of the Garth Valley Hunt, the working day had started before the night had ended as the elderly huntsman prepared the pack for another morning's cubbing. In the hilly, rough, mountainous country, horses were of only a limited use and many supporters would follow on foot, gaining vantage points where the work of the hounds could best be followed. In his seventeenth season as huntsman, Lewis started down the lane, followed by his coupled hounds, reaching fitness and eager for the morning's sport. The great, shaggy-coated Welsh hounds, under close control, had some way to go, and the huntsman stepped out smartly with Ruby and Dana and Traveller and Teifi close at his heels, leading their kennelmates. There had been too many foxes in the woods on their last visit and Lewis has been far from satisfied. They must work it again, more thoroughly, to thin them out and split them up, scattering them to the four winds and culling the runts to ensure better sport for the season. He knew that many foxes had skulked through the undergrowth and the old vixen which had taken the pack away had foiled the purpose of their visit. They would hunt through it once more. It was an ideal training ground for the young hounds.

The dog fox was instantly awake and alert.

Raising himself slowly, he strained his ears and again, faintly, came the sound that had aroused him. The sharp note of the hunting horn rose above the far off voices of the pack and he knew that he was, once again, in the presence of his enemies. A slight breeze carried their scent to his nostrils and he lingered no more. Leaving the shelter of the thorns, he followed a ditch until he came to a shallow stream and, crossing it, he padded warily along a footpath which brought him to a wide lane. He hesitated, listening. The pack was still hunting in the forest, running with a cry which sent him a message of doom even though they were far behind him. He turned from the lane through a gap in the hedge and, quickening his pace, moved steadily across country, leaving the wood and its fears, far behind. Soon he had out-reached the call of the hunting horn and, by midday, he had left the land of the Garth Valley Hunt. He did not know that his sister had also been driven away and had escaped in another direction. They would never meet again. The pack had claimed another two lives that morning, running one young fox to ground, and had caused many more to disperse seeking other territories, roaming independently and leaving the forest, which could not support an over-large fox population with safety.

The dog fox, out of danger, rested. He had hunted and scavenged all the night and travelled for hours that day and

Instantly awake and alert.

though he was three miles from the forest, in his wanderings he had covered a much greater distance to reach his present position. He looked about him and started towards a marshland, heavily covered with scrub. The boggy surface could barely support his weight in places and he was glad when he had crossed it for it made a precarious resting place. He saw some buildings ahead and heard the sound of hens, and his curiosity took him forward. Soon he peered through a thick hedge and saw the poultry clearly. He was hungry again. Stealthily approaching a small gap, he forced his head and shoulders through and became aware of a constriction at his throat. In panic, he withdrew, pulling away sharply, but he found himself firmly held. Thrashing about in fear, the wire took hold even more firmly and he began to choke. Soon he could struggle no more for every move simply increased the pressure and he felt as if his lungs were tearing in their fight for breath. He lay still. What further misfortune was this?

As twilight approached, the noose eased, cutting less tightly, and he barked at the night. The forlorn sound echoed in the shadows and the mocking cries of the evening rang in his ears. Somewhere, a living thing screeched its life away as stoat or weasel found a victim, and the small animals of the hedgerow shuffled about in the gloom. Again he barked, and again, but no one cared or seemed to notice.

Silence had descended on the henhouse and all sat safely on their perches, brown heads still and motionless. A hedgehog moved along the ditch and pressed its snout to the leaf mould and the fox barked once more and now, in his sorrow, he wished to bark forever. He told the stars of his misfortune, he called to his ancestors and cried for their advice, he cursed the world for his troubles and he mourned at the fate which had given him life as a fox. His cries did not go unheeded.

The door of the farmhouse opened, letting a yellow glow into the night and, pulling on his coat, Elwyn Morgan signalled his sheep dog to heel, took up his hurricane lamp, and crossed the yard to the henhouse. After securing the chickens he would attend to the fox which he had snared and which called incessantly for the mercy of a swift death.

He parted the thorny branches and peered at the fox. The animal was frightened, but returned his gaze and hissed, with teeth bared in its open jaws, fangs showing. Elwyn's cur-dog barked excitedly and darted in and out, keeping well away from the danger and the farmer poked at the captive with a heavy stick. The sudden lightning snap made him jump, and he could not help but admire the beauty and bravery of the beast which he had trapped. He stood, for long moments, as the fox, jaws wide, crouched ready to retaliate and he raised his club to strike at it, but he did not.

He had trapped many foxes, for he was adept in the use of a snare. Usually they were dead when he found them and if they were not he would soon kill them, but now he hesitated and the seed of an unusual idea came to him. This was a fine animal, a prime specimen. Big, but young. He wondered if he could tame it, domesticate it, turn it into a pet. He decided to take the fox alive. He fumbled in his pocket for some string and when he had unravelled a length he approached the animal cautiously. He thrust his stick again at the prisoner and it was seized immediately, in the powerful, clamping jaws, and held fast. It was a grip so hard that the gums began to bleed, as Morgan, deftly and hastily, tied the muzzle with his string. Too late to struggle now and release the stick, the cord was made secure and knotted once more behind the head. Unfastening the snare from its anchoring branch, Elwyn dragged the struggling fox from its prison and carried it back to the farm. The sheep dog, now made brave, lunged at the helpless form but was met by Elwyn's boot and slunk away. He called to his son and together they entered the barn and opened the lid of a stone-built feed storage bin. While Elwyn held the fox firmly at the back of the head, his son removed the snare and cut away the restricting twine. The fox hung from strong hands, jaws agape, voiding his body in fear, as the two men admired him, talking and joking. Elwyn lowered him into the bin and threw him to a corner, quickly closing the heavy lid and securing it with the clasp. In the cold darkness, the fox settled, fearfully and defensively, into his corner. It would be a long night, filled with apprehension.

But not for Elwyn Morgan.

He had slept soundly.

He had exhausted himself in his wife's embrace and had then hardly stirred, breathing deeply and heavily, all tension removed from his hard body. When he awoke, he was relaxed and calm and in a good humour. A simple man, without inner conflict. A man sure of himself and sure of his lifestyle. He attended to his duties and provided for his family. He had no hobbies, spent hardly any time drinking at the inn, and asked for little from the world. He loved the land and its living and, in his own quiet way, gloried in his ability to wring from it the necessities for his simple life. The fate of fox or badger, rat or rabbit, or indeed, any wild thing, caused him no anxiety. He was not a man without pity but he would not waste it on anything that could threaten his prosperity. He sang at the little chapel, with a strong, manly baritone voice and when the preacher, quoting from the good book, gave man dominion over all, he could see no reason to disagree, with him or his God. He saved his sympathy for his family, his friends, his neighbours and his relatives. He would help any in misfortune, he would come to the assistance of those in distress and he would give generously to those in despair, provided their circumstances were due to ill luck and not of their own making. He lived, as he liked to say, a Christian life, and his open face and contented manner plainly advertised the fact. He was a kindly man, well thought of by all, and one who had earned the respect his fellows accorded him.

The fox was his enemy and did not qualify to be treated according to the principles that otherwise ruled his life and so, that afternoon, when he carefully lifted the heavy lid of the food bin and gazed down on the fine, but forlorn figure crouched in the corner, he felt no pity, no remorse. He still pondered the fate of the fox. He did not know the reason for his action of the previous evening. Normally he would simply end the life of a captive and reset the snare. Now he was uncertain of his course. The fox eyed him with foreboding and Elwyn was careful not to raise the lid too far. One quick spring and the fox would be free for he could have easily cleared the high sided bin even though he felt a stiffness in his limbs, due to his confinement in the cold prison. Elwyn would give him no such chance.

"Kill the bugger, dad", said his son, and Elwyn admonished him swiftly for his coarse language. Together, they soon restrained the animal and fastened a stout collar tightly about his throat, clipping it to a strong chain, used normally to tether the farm dogs to their kennels. The fox, unused to such restriction, tried frantically to break free, hurling itself into the air and biting in terror at the chain, until his gums bled.

It was all in vain.

Try as he may, there could be no escape and Elwyn, now sure of his captive, attached the free end of the chain to a secure bracket which had been driven into the wall of the barn. The fox paced restlessly to the limits of the chain, hating the collar and the metallic clinking sound that accompanied his every move, seeking in vain to regain the freedom he had so carelessly lost.

He would never be tamed.

He was a son of the wilderness and would never surrender to existence in a cage, or submit to restraint.

One chance.

One more chance.

He would be ready when it came.

Elwyn Morgan, watching the animal, sensed this. He could plainly see the proud independence now bound, symbolically, by a strong collar. He felt in his bones that he would never come to dominate such a creature but Elwyn loved a challenge. He was at his best when faced with a problem. The easy, monotonous tasks held no attraction for him, but he never could ignore the lure of something new, something difficult.

And so he set out to tame his fox.

He began by depriving him of food and then, feeding gradually and slowly and with quiet words and easy movements, he hoped to gain the confidence of his prisoner. Days became weeks and an uneasy truce developed almost into an acceptance, a tolerance and yet, it was, essentially, almost.

Elwyn dared not remove the collar and even though the fox now followed for walks on the long chain, their relationship was still one of mistrust. Elwyn had even given his prisoner a name by now and the fox had soon begun to associate it with food.

Cadno. The ancient Welsh word for fox. He used it every time he approached and soon the word would bring the captive out of his kennel. Weeks had gone by and still Cadno was not to be trusted. Elwyn could feed him and touch him, but never would the cold, yellow eyes soften, never would any friendship show in them. The luxurious brush would wave in the air at the scent of a meal but this was merely a reflex pleasure action and owed nothing to the actual presence of the provider. Cadno would spend all his time in the confines of his kennel prison, his horizons restricted by the smaller length of chain to which he had, by now, been fastened. The place became daily more foul and foetid as the bedding on which he lay, and the ground where he paced, putrified to the pollution of his bodily wastes.

He was rarely walked now, or even spoken to, as the challenge became more hopeless, and sometimes days would pass before some scrap of food would be brought. Cadno became more morose and even unpredictable and once, when his rush from the kennel startled his jailer, Elwyn kicked at him, his heavy boot thudding into his head and sending Cadno, stunned, to the floor.

He was becoming a nuisance.

He would have to die.

At the bottom of the yard, a dry stone drain, disused and broken, ran for fourteen feet and ended in a small recess, and Elwyn Morgan took Cadno and threw him roughly in, covering the recess with a wooden lid. His son was ready at the drain entrance, and loosed a small white terrier at his father's command. The bitch disappeared into the drain.

Cadno had, instinctively, adopted a defensive attitude as soon as he was dropped into the recess, aware only that his neck was no longer banded by a collar, but knowing that his ordeal was not yet over. Soon he could hear the approach of the terrier as it moved through the drain and then his ears were assailed by the shrill barks, screams almost, of his new tormentor. In the darkness, the small bitch darted and pranced and bayed and still Cadno crouched, motionless, unsure of himself with his jaws gaping wide. Soon the terrier grew bolder approaching to within inches of the fox and Cadno heard the sudden, deafening stamping of heavy boots on the wooden cover above him. Agitated by this new threat from his human captor, he hurled himself forward and his strong jaws struck the bitch above the eye, gouting blood all over her face. He followed up his attack, knowing he had an advantage and the terrier bundled backwards, retreating bleeding, out of the drain. Morgan was amazed. He gathered up the bitch and, just in time, thrust his boot into the drain as the head of Cadno appeared, prepared to make a bolt for his freedom. Elwyn dragged a heavy stone to block the exit and placed another on top of the wooden cover above the recess. The terrier was covered in her own blood where Cadno had pierced her foreface and ripped at her eye and ear. Morgan washed her down with cold water at the stream and took her back to the kennel, returning with her father, an older, wiser dog, one that had worked fox before, and knew what to expect.

The dog entered more warily than his daughter, but this time he did not reach the end of the drain. Before he had gone half way, Cadno met him head on and a tremendous scuffle took place. Soon the terrier's barks turned to cries of pain and he, too, was forced to retreat, followed to the entrance once more by his furious opponent. It had all happened so quickly. Elwyn Morgan smiled. He could have a lot of fun from such a fox, and earn some money too. Making sure that there was no escape for Cadno, he returned to the kennel with his defeated terrier, and finished his work for the day.

That evening he made one of his rare visits to the inn, where he told of the terrible power of his prisoner.

A fox that feared no terrier.

A fox that drove terriers out of the ground.

Anyone who wished to try their terriers to such an animal could do so.

There were plenty of takers.

Practically every farm and every home had a terrier of sorts. They killed rats, marked rabbits. Some were used for foxes and a few, even to badgers. They varied in ability and courage. Some had never worked below ground on their own, showing their ability only when accompanied by another dog, and others were terriers that would bay well, but not too closely to their quarry. A few, a select few, were dogs of quality. Reliable, experienced, fox killers, even.

Cadno dealt with them all. So violent was his reaction that some terriers were met only a few feet from the entrance and bundled out unceremoniously. Others would be allowed almost into the recess, as if Cadno cared nothing for their presence, then he would burst into explosive action. Many terriers were thoroughly trounced, fleeing in haste. Some gave up only after a great battle, but none were able to defeat the fox. Indeed, only one *would* be allowed to defeat him, for every time he fought, he fought, unknowingly, for his life. To lose would be to die. He was well fed and well cared for. He became valuable to Elwyn Morgan.

Cadno became famed and nothing was asked of him except when he was taken to the drain. All thoughts of taming the animal had gone. He would never be tamed. He was wilder than ever and would always be wild. Though they had given him a name, he would never belong to them. He would never be their property. But he was not free.

Chapter 6

Bruiser

Tom rose from his bed early, as was his habit. It was not yet dawn and he groped about, lighting a candle and setting the fire, waiting for the day to make its appearance. It was his birthday but it made no difference. Life begins at forty, he thought wryly, so he had a few years to go. It had begun again for him when he came to the cottage, so he would not have to wait until he was forty. It was 1935 and though he paid little attention to the news of the day, he could not help be aware that Europe was again on the road to turmoil as a madman raved in Germany.

Satisfied as he saw the sticks slowly crackle into flame in the grate, he opened the door of his cottage and stood, silently, looking over the fields. The mist had not yet risen and clung eerily to the land like a shroud as the first light gently pushed aside the darkness. Nothing stirred, and the sheep across the meadow made a strange sight. Covered from feet to flank by the ground mist, they appeared as motionless, bodiless heads resting gloomily above a cotton wool cloud. Further along, the foothills climbed away from the greyness and the woodland, dark and moody, stood out sharply. He thought of his neighbour, a mile away, who had come to him the previous evening, rambling on about the sign of a Corpse Candle. It foretold death, he had said, and he had seen it hovering outside his door when he opened it in the early morning. It appeared again when darkness fell, moving toward him as if to claim him. He had slammed the door shut and ran from the house at the rear entrance, hurrying to bring the bad news to Tom. He was doomed and had not long to live. Tom had calmed him as best he could, serving him a mixture of whisky, sugar and warm water and it had settled the old man's nerves. His superstitions were strong, a potent mixture of religion and myth, and Tom feared that the day would soon come when he would have to be taken away from the lonely life he led on his small farm. He walked home with him across the fields and stayed with him until he was calmer. As his eyes swept over the scene before him, Tom could understand how the old people reverted to the legends of the past, stories told to them as children and passed from generation to generation. Stories of magic and witchcraft, of wizards and ghosts and strange characters from strange worlds. He shivered as he washed himself quickly, not entirely due to the shock of the cold water, and he soaped his ears and rinsed behind them as his mother had taught him so often, so many years ago. Why should he be thinking of her, after all this time? He had lost contact with his father and his sister and it did not bother him. Yet, his mother came often to his mind. He rubbed himself briskly with the rough, coarse towel which he had fashioned from a close-woven sack and then he stood in front of the fire, drying himself thoroughly with a proper towel and watching the steam which had already started to hiss from the big black kettle.

Bruiser stretched, and moved slowly from the bedroom, scratching at the door, waiting to go out to the fields to lift his leg. Tom patted his head and opened the door, leaving it ajar for his return. He would not be long. He liked to be in the house at breakfast time.

Tom dressed, lacing on his heavy boots, as bacon sizzled in the pan, and as breakfast cooked, Bruiser wandered back to the fire, waiting patiently for the few scraps he knew would be his. It was a hunting morning and as soon as the meal was cleared, Tom made his way to the meet. He had coupled Bruiser with an older bitch, taken as insurance, should the young terrier be unable to do his job. So far the veteran had not been needed. Bruiser had passed every test and had proven himself equal to all situations and though the season was only half way through he was already making his reputation.

Bruiser.

The followers had looked upon the black terriers with suspicion at first, for they had never seen their like before. Tom had started his strain with three terriers purchased when he had fought in Durham.

His interest in terrier sport was well known and whenever his contests took him north, he could usually arrange to do some digging after the bout. He was very popular with the northern sportsmen, miners like himself mostly, and hard men from the heavy industries of steel and shipbuilding who admired his fiery, game, battling style.

After the Durham contest he had spent some time with terriermen in Yorkshire and had been particularly impressed with the animals of a tall, gaunt, well spoken man, something of a legend in his locality. He bred a very capable and intelligent strain and Tom had been so persistent with his requests that the man had sold him a bitch pup. Three months later, the man had sent him, by rail, another bitch pup, and also a red dog of some three seasons' experience and Bruiser had been bred from these animals, which had proven themselves over the years.

The hounds had set off from their kennels before Tom left his house, for today they would meet only a mile away from Tom's cottage, at a small farmhouse where many lambs had been lost at the end of the season's hunting. The huntsman had a seven mile journey and he led his pack across country and along lanes from the kennel until he arrived at a crossroad leading on to the main highway. He met two more horsemen awaiting his arrival and these men took up their positions behind the hounds as they continued along the road. The bay mare settled into a steady stride and the hounds, all in leather couples close at her heels, eased into their rhythm, sterns carried well, eager to start the day. They were fully fit and as disciplined as a Welsh foxhound pack could ever be and most of the younger hounds had entered well, revelling in their first season. Raleigh and Raglan, Gelert and Bowman, Delyth and Dinam, the young entry were well into their stride and proving the value of their ancient bloodlines. They would not be uncoupled until they reached their destination, for to do so earlier would mean that the pack could be likely to split up and go off hunting on their own.

Tom had left his yard at the back gate and climbed the hill, passing near the edge of the woods and though the mist had dispersed with the slight breeze, the mossy turf beneath his feet remained heavy and caused him to slip, until he reached the stony path. After a steady climb, he could look down over the river's course and saw it twisting and turning along the valley floor. Movement in the distance showed him the route of the hounds and, turning about, he saw three of four horses waiting, restlessly, already at the meet. Tom arrived only minutes before the hounds, who were soon sniffing about at the terriers, who warily accepted the attentions of their much larger partners. He was always pleased to see this. It meant there would be much less chance of an accident, should a fox and a terrier bolt, as one, from a warren, and in his many seasons he had never once known the hounds to make a mistake with his dogs. They knew their scent too well.

After a period of banter and chatter, the huntsman moved to the rough road which led up to the hillside, passing above the farm, and the mounted followers positioned themselves where they could best follow the expected proceedings. Tom stood near a dilapidated barn which looked as if it would not withstand the next high wind, and he found himself in the company of an old gamekeeper from the estate, who offered to carry some of the tools. Tom was pleased to have his assistance and gave him the bar and the heavy ceib, or mattock, carrying his two spades fastened across his shoulder with a stout rope. Gathering up his terriers from their tether at a gate post, he hurried to keep up with the hunt, in the company of his new acquaintance.

The pack were eager and keen, knowing their enemy had been abroad during the night and, crossing the second field, deep-throated Ranger began to speak, harmonised immediately by the lighter soprano voices of Ruby and Dana as the experienced bitches took up the cry, the full pack now coming to chorus.

Over the fields, two foxes were viewed and the stronger was soon running well, outstripping his smaller companion who was being rapidly overhauled by Dana. Into a bracken patch and out of sight now, but the hounds were close and the short run came to an abrupt end. The pack were marking to ground. Lewis, the huntsman, was quickly at the scene and, as he had expected, found Ruby tightly wedged into the entrance of the earth. Sounding three blasts on the horn, he called for terriers, but he had no intention of wasting his time at the awkward bury. He was looking forward to a good chase and hoped the strong, first fox would provide it. Leaving one of the whips to mark the earth and follow on later, he soon had the hounds in full cry, away across the hill, on the scent of the larger fox.

Arriving at the earth, Tom fastened his terriers to a stout branch in the hedge and looked about him, studying the scene. His first, cursory glance showed that two holes had been opened but he carefully examined the area and found three more entrances, half filled with leaves and brittle brown bracken. He spent some time gathering fallen timber to block these possible escape routes and then turned his attention to the two entrances which had been excavated. Ruby, in her rage, had almost blocked off the smaller hole and Tom cleared the loose soil which the eager hound had collapsed in her anxiety to reach the fox. And as he did so, the gamekeeper arrived and blocked the remaining hole, digging at the earth above the entrance with the mattock. Piles of old bracken and grass and moss had been dragged out of the tunnels and lay strewn about, mixed with the earth at the entrances where Tom now stood. He hoped that the badger which had aired this bedding had moved on to take up residence elsewhere. Bruiser had not yet worked to brock and Tom wanted the young dog to settle down and lose some of his impetuosity as he gained experience, before entering to badger and even then, he planned to arrange the first encounter for a small, easy-to-dig sett. He considered using the older terrier, just in case Brock was still at home but decided, instead, to continue with the education of the young protege.

As he released the terrier from the coupling, he noticed that the wind, rising sharply, had changed both its directions and its nature. The hedge no longer offered a shelter, and the day took on a decided chill as Bruiser, eager to seek out his quarry, entered the earth.

Tom lay on the ground with his head and shoulders thrust into the hole but, after fifteen minutes, he had still not heard even the faintest sound. With his first misgivings, he realised that the sett was bigger than he had expected and he now began to check, ear to the ground, for sounds of the terrier, testing many places, while the gamekeeper guarded the entrance.

A robin hopped through the hedge, his small face alert and bewildered and, as if curious, he remained in the area as the day progressed, often perching high on the hedge and surveying his little kingdom. As if well pleased, he sang his delicate song, the notes as liquid and transparent as the ice-cold waters of the murmuring brook.

After an hour, there was still no sound to be heard from the earth and the freezing wind from the west coast chilled Tom's face after its thousand mile journey from far out in the Atlantic ocean, stinging into his face and forcing tear drops from his eyes as it searched out every weakness in his clothing.

The hounds had long since passed out of earshot and as mid-day approached, Tom and the keeper reviewed their situation. It was possible that Bruiser had met with an accident for surely, by now, some sound, some stirring, would have filtered through to them. The dog would bay with a voice like a brass bell when close to a fox and he would have to be deep into the earth for all sound to be stifled. Tom cursed silently, regretting his decision to enter the dog but it had not appeared to be a difficult earth in any way and he knew that really, he had no cause to blame himself. He considered letting the older terrier loose but it was a practice he tried to avoid and he would indeed by a desperate man to let another terrier join Bruiser in this deceptive bury. He would have to wait, and so, he began, once more, to move about, listening intently, ear pressed to the ground, desperately straining for some sound to register through the background noise of the wind as it busied itself about the hedge.

The old keeper had abandoned his watch at the entrance, blocking it partially, and seeking some shelter crouched at a bend in the hedge and it was he who now called the terrierman's attention to the slight tremor beneath his feet. Tom lay with his head near the entrance and, at first, ignored the man. He was fifty yards away, much too far, the earth did not extend there, surely? He pretended not to hear the calls and then in his frustration, he carried the bar to the sheltered spot to humour the old man and his ridiculous claim. Even before he lay on the ground, he could hear his terrier far below, baying strongly, deep in the earth. He thrust at the ground with the bar, forcing it as far into the soil as it could go and listening at each hole as he withdrew it. Soon he marked the spot where the sound of the terrier could be heard most clearly and now, cheered with a new hope, he began to dig.

The earth was hard, and rocky, and after a steady hour at work with the spade, he had only managed a small trench about three feet deep. Numerous thick roots blocked the way through and it was a time consuming job to clear the hole, cutting through each root with the mattock and the edge of the shovel blade. He tried the bar again, forcing it deep into the ground and though he could hear the terrier more plainly, the sound of his barking was still muffled by the earth. The deeper he dug, the harder it became to throw out the loose soil and, at a depth of seven feet, the light began to fade rapidly as dusk approached. The digging would soon have to stop for the day. It was 4.30 and Bruiser, still baying powerfully, had been hard at it for almost six hours. There was little more that could be done and, after waiting another two hours, Tom and the keeper placed branches loosely across the entrance and, in complete darkness, left the mountain for the night. Bruiser was still baying steadily.

That evening, Tom's small cottage seemed strangely empty and silent without the little terrier and, sitting close to the hearth as the wind moaned about the building, Tom ate his evening meal deep in thought. The night, though now dry, was cold and the chill wind kept all indoors but, after eating his supper, Tom returned to the deep hole he had dug that day. Approaching in silence, he dropped lightly into the excavation and, laying with his ear pressed tight to the soil, he heard the booming tones of Bruiser, still engaging the enemy. He stayed there for another hour before leaving and he knew that if the terrier emerged, he would find his way home without difficulty. Tom went to his bed a tired, but satisfied man. He did not expect Bruiser to return home that night and planned to be back on the hill at first light, to continue the dig.

He slept with a troubled mind. More than once he jerked wildly awake with dreamlike images still burned into his restless brain. Why? He had many times left terriers to work overnight, it was nothing new. He awoke once with visions of his mother, confined in a cage like a wild beast and clawing at the bars, shouting and screaming wildly as the cage was bounced down a steep slope, sinking eventually into the filthy, putrid mud of a Flanders battlefield. The bars opened, and she sprang out, attacking him savagely with a long knife. Another time, he saw his father, calling to him in vain for rescue as, bound tight with ivy boughs, he was carried off by phantom creatures with wings and skeletal, wasted tails. He was not an imaginative man, to indulge in flights of fancy, and these images left him shattered, mentally and physically exhausted, until, well before dawn, he rose from his bed with every picture still vividly before him. Throughout his childhood, he had been raised and lived, to treat animals with care and kindness and all his life as a hunter would be spent in a ceaseless, inner conflict. He felt for his victims, identified with them, pushed guilty thoughts to the back of his mind, out of sight, but at times of stress or anxiety, he could not keep them submerged. He knew that he fought a never-ending battle with his conscience, he could never totally resign himself to his chosen lifestyle. Though he hated the killing, he loved the sport and knew it to be vital and essential to the rural community. He loved the little, game terriers and the relentless great hounds. He loved the victors and he loved the victims. He pushed his conflicts, once again, to the dark cellars of his brain, hidden for another day and then, washing quickly to freshen himself, he prepared for the work ahead.

With first light still some time away, he set off over the damp fields, pulling his muffler about his throat and ears and raising its edge to protect his nose from the wind. It had rained during the night but now dawn came clear and bright, but cold, and the sharp wind in his face made him turn away as he climbed to the mountain top before making his way down to the diggings of yesterday. Dropping into the pit, he lay once more, listening intently. At least it was sheltered from the noise and sting of the wind but, in the relative quiet, he could hear nothing. He pushed the bar into the ground and, withdrawing it, pressed his ear to the hole.

Silence.

He called down into the earth.

Bruiser. Bruiser. Good boy. Bruiser.

Nothing.

He checked the entrance, still carefully covered with branches and undisturbed. Bruiser was down there in the earth and so was his foe but perhaps, he thought, they may have moved to another section of the sett. He lowered himself once more into the huge hole and prodded the bar diagonally into the bank. Faintly, he caught a distinct rasp of hoarse barking. The terrier was still at work, but now he had moved even further into the maze of passages. For an hour, Tom kept on digging down, tunnelling into the bank, steadily and without haste, pacing himself for a long day, filling every spade stroke and conserving his energy for the task before him. When next he stopped to listen, the sound of the conflict seemed to be clearer. He was making progress.

The day developed free of any cloud though the wind still whipped over the hill and Tom, taking a breather, huddled in the bracken for shelter as he looked down to the farm in the valley, far below. Three men were climbing towards him, coming slowly up the rough sheep track, and, as they approached, he saw Lewis, the huntsman, with his eldest son Gareth and, bringing up the rear, the old gamekeeper. Soon they had crossed the dry-stone wall and were on the open mountain, hiding from the wind whenever they could by following undulating ridges. As Tom waited, he saw the robin, yesterday's inquisitive spectator, still watching as it foraged, approaching often and peering intently with his sharp, bright eyes, looking himself, like a tiny huntsman in his scarlet, feathered waistcoat.

The men wasted little time in idle chatter and, dropping into the excavation, Gareth and his father were soon at work, digging steadily, with Tom behind, clearing away the soil which they threw to the rear. About two hours later, the men called Tom forward and when he burrowed his way into the bank and prodded carefully with his bar, he finally found the chamber where Bruiser, at the close proximity of his master, worked with renewed urgency. Clearing the loose soil and enlarging the hole, the terrier could be seen baying into the darkness as Tom inched his way behind him, widening the hole with his bare hands.

The strong scent of fox filled the little passageway but another, even more heavy smell, came to his nostrils. Screwing up his eyes and squinting into the half light of the tunnel, Tom saw that Bruiser lay on top of a fox and, probing gently, he pulled the animal from beneath the terrier. It was indeed a fine fox, big, strong and red, and quite dead. Not the animal that Tom and the huntsman had seen run into the ground before hounds on the previous day. Opening out the earth still further he could see another lifeless fox and this appeared to be the fugitive of yesterday.

Withdrawing this victim, he passed both bodies behind him and turned once more to the terrier, now intent on the animal before him.

Tom knew it was a badger and hoped that the terrier would not be too rash. He was far too useful to come to grief in a battle with brock. Seizing his tail, he drew Bruiser, writhing and struggling, from the earth and, holding him as quietly as he was able, saw two large badgers charge from the earth, careering down the mountain slope with a speed which surprised the men on the hill and losing themselves from sight in the bracken before a shot could be fired after them. Still Bruiser squirmed and his master, with some trepidation, returned him to the workings where he inched cautiously into the space vacated by the badgers. Soon he was yapping again, steadily, but after a short time the barking stopped and Bruiser's tail appeared, the little animal tugging and straining as he hauled out yet another dead fox.

There were two badgers in the earth.

He had accounted for three foxes and had also worked two badgers which stood between him and his final victim. He had set himself a standard from which he would never be expected to descend. The life of the legend had begun to unfold in earnest.

Tom and his companions backfilled the crater they had dug and made their way down to the farmhouse where the heavy kettle steamed on the hob in the kitchen. They cleaned Bruiser and bathed his face and muzzle though his injuries were, surprisingly, few. He was exhausted rather than damaged and, after eating a small meal, he lay on the floor, close to the brass-bound fender, basking in the heat from the large peat fire as the men ate the dishes of warm broth and bread and cheese placed before them.

Finishing their meal, they huddled about the fire in the inglenook of the large kitchen and they drank a glass of whisky as they marvelled at the courage and tenacity which had enabled the little terrier to carry out such an enormous task, and they praised him wholeheartedly. They stayed on, drinking home-made wine and talking but eventually, they parted and went their separate ways.

Tom, alone, walked back over the mountain to his cottage, carrying all the tools on his shoulder but feeling them to be no burden. His step was light and his manner carefree and sometimes he would burst into a tuneless song. His terrier followed, dourly, in his master's footsteps, never more than a yard or two behind though a great tiredness had begun to settle upon his rapidly stiffening muscles.

Chapter 7

A Bargain is Struck

Elwyn Morgan almost lost Cadno.

He thought the fox to be just about invincible in his drain, and had full confidence in its ability to trounce any terrier and so he was not unduly concerned when he allowed a forty pound bull terrier to squeeze into the narrow entrance. If the fox had remained in the recess he would have been safe but, true to form, he hurried to meet the new intruder. The bull terrier screamed with rage and pain as the long, sharp fangs pierced his muzzle, but he did not retreat. One reason was that he was jammed tight, the other reason being that pain and aggression only served to rouse him to a fury. His strong jaws searched vainly for a grip but at last, his powerful struggles forced the fox to release its hold and the enormous mouth grasped the fur at the top of Cadno's head.

The terrier had no room to move and could not shake his victim and Cadno, wrenching himself free, escaped and retreated, feeling intense pain as one velvet ear was torn from the top of his head. The terrier heaved mightily and forced his bulging body through the drain and Morgan, sensing disaster, quickly removed the wooden cover and caught Cadno at the throat with a large tongs, lifting the creature to safety and further captivity, for further torment.

He was rested then and Elwyn Morgan refused all combat requests until Cadno was fully recovered, using the time to modify the drain, allowing access only to terriers of a proper size. One month later, the challenges resumed and Cadno seemed to have become even more reckless and savage.

His life had become one of despair for so proud an animal. He was fed well, but irregularly, whenever his captor felt like it and, due to Morgan's indifference, was confined in foul and increasingly verminous quarters. Day or night were as one to the young fox, and the sounds of the fields and the farm only served to increase his misery. In his hopelessness, he cared not if he lived or died and his battles with his many tormentors seemed to offer his only chance of escape.

Tom Flanders had heard tales of the famous fox and had disbelieved most of them, for the telling had added to the feats until it seemed to be a magical creature. Tom had no time for such activities but nevertheless, his curiosity and interest in all things canine and vulpine, brought him to Morgan's farm, accompanied by Bruiser.

He looked at the fox, cowering in his kennel of filth, and he knew pity.

He looked at the drain, and the recess with its lid, and he knew anger.

He looked at the bland, honest face of Elwyn Morgan and felt bewilderment and could not understand how such a man, so decent in all other respects, should treat an animal so callously and carelessly, though he knew that mere man is a creature of many moods and facets and is able to alter his attitude to embrace every circumstance.

He offered to buy the fox, but Morgan would not hear of it. He enjoyed his notoriety and fame. Cadno had earned him a tidy sum and would continue to do so until he was killed. He suspected that Tom Flanders would like to own Cadno, to take over his role.

No sale.

He could try his terrier and pay if he lost. If Cadno were killed, then Morgan would pay. Tom made a further condition. If he could save the fox from certain death, Cadno would be his, if he failed, he would double the payment to Morgan. The fox was placed in the recess at the end of the drain. The lid was secured above him.

Tom removed Bruiser's collar and chain and carried him to the drain entrance.

The terrier sniffed into the dank darkness and moved cautiously forward, pushing into the now restricted space with his muscular, rear legs. When he was halfway along he became aware of the fox moving towards him, and he began to bay.

Cadno struck at him and sliced the muzzle at the side, splitting a gum and Bruiser retaliated with a controlled but terrible violence, driving the fox backwards, towards his recess. The sound of the bloody combat rose to a crescendo as Bruiser watched for his chance and then only a subdued angry growling and scuffling could be heard. Morgan lifted the lid and saw that Bruiser held Cadno securely at the throat, squeezing his life away.

Tom stepped forward, pushing Morgan roughly aside, and lifted the animals clear. He hurried to his cart and placed the limp fox into a mesh-fronted box and then he felt for Bruiser's windpipe, squeezing and cutting off the air supply until the terrier was forced to relinquish his grip. He closed and bolted the lid of the box and fastened Bruiser to his tether.

Morgan, misreading his intentions and conveniently forgetting the bargain, thanked him profusely for saving Cadno, but Tom pressed two pound notes into his hand and drove away, paying even though he had won, and taking Cadno and Bruiser with him. Elwyn Morgan followed behind the card until they reached the gate and there Tom stopped and dismounted. He was still in full control of himself and this made him all the more menacing and Morgan knew that he was beaten. Shouting threats, and using oaths which he had forbidden to his son, he retreated to his farmhouse, watching the cart as it slowly moved away, until it was out of sight.

Tom, though outwardly calm, was seething with rage and he allowed himself two miles of slow progress before he felt his tension ease. He stopped the cart and tied Bruiser's leash to a wheel and then he opened the box. Cadno met his eye without apparent fear and his torn ear gave him an odd appearance of toughness. He seemed to care little for Tom's intentions and still he stared at his new captor. Suddenly Tom's hand stretched out, and he grasped the fox firmly behind the head. Before Cadno could react, he was securely held and Tom examined him closely. Apart from his ear, he appeared to be free from any serious injury, though his foreface bore several scars from his battles, and his throat bled slightly from Bruiser's vice-like grip. The teeth were all intact and gleamed, shining white, and though his rich, russet fur lacked lustre, this was due to his conditions of captivity and would soon shine again. He was one of the biggest foxes Tom had ever seen, and he guessed his weight, accurately, at about twenty-four pounds. The head was large, almost wolf-like, and the fangs curved menacingly like the blades of wicked scimitars. Added to this, his unnatural manner of indifference, rather than fear, made Tom believe that perhaps many of the stories told about him were true. Cadno would be a fox to give any pack a run and, in a familiar bury, it would take a better than average terrier to best him.

Cadno was almost wolf-like.

Tom carried him to the side of the road, and crossed into a field, clambering over an old stile. He held Cadno before him and threw him gently forward. As his feet touched the grass, the fox sped away, glancing behind, as if unable to believe that he was not being pursued, and relishing again the freedom he had so long yearned for. At a safe distance, he stopped, and turned to stare at Tom for a full minute, as if trying to fathom the actions of the man, and then he made off, across the field. Soon he was lost to sight, but he was on his way back to the dense woodlands he had left so many moons before.

Tom hoped he would make good use of his liberty and sire some strong cubs, but he realised that his action could have serious consequences. Such a fox could be a terrible problem. Such a fox would be easily capable of killing a lamb and, due to his period of captivity could, perhaps, show scant respect for the presence of man. It was too late now, Tom had taken a calculated risk. The fox had earned a spell of freedom and Tom hoped that he would make the most of it without causing any trouble. Cadno had been a prisoner for many months and had seen action against a good many cur-type terriers.

He returned to the cart and drove home, with Bruiser sniffing inquisitively at the scent which clung to his hands and clothes.

Cadno did not stop until he gained the shelter of the wood and then he lay, safe and secure and free, in the same dense bramble and bracken that had hidden him on his last night of liberty, so long ago, it seemed to him. He wallowed in filth and rolled in carrion, he groomed himself incessantly and cleaned himself in grass and rushes until, at last, he felt himself to be free of the awful scent of man, his enemy, and the scourge of his kind.

As he rid himself of the tainted scent he hated, so he threw off the memory of his time in the custody of Elwyn Morgan. He relished the wide world which was now his and he roamed as he pleased, coming into contact with all the other animals, which took for granted the wildness which Cadno had, for so long, so carelessly lost.

Chapter 8

Freedom

After his release, Cadno had roamed the land with added caution.

He was determined never to lose again, the freedom he had been born for, and his wanderings took him to the wild mountains where man rarely ventured.

He had spent all the summer months in the hills and did not intend to forsake their safety. Though food was not plentiful, he survived by cunning and hard hunting and rarely knew real hunger, but as autumn came to his mountain home, so his living became harder.

The days were short and the season chilled and soon the angry storms of winter forced him to move on. He retraced his footsteps, returning to the land of bitter memories, but it was a land of relative plenty where at least, a fox could find an easier meal and mix with those of his own species.

It was early December and the wintry sun had made a spectacle of itself, sinking like a furious orange fireball from the leaden grey, cold, early evening sky, and Cadno went a courting.

Screams and barks and tell-tale scenting spots drew him like a magnet to the gently sloping fields bordering the river where, among the brambles and rhododendron's and brown bracken, two second season vixens lived in friendly maidenhood. Their dam had been killed by hounds after a lamb worrying escapade in early April, but since that awful day, the sisters had been left alone, undisturbed, to enjoy the changing seasons. Soon, they would approach the mating condition, and they welcomed the arrival of Cadno who, for the first time since the day he had last seen his mother and sister, roamed freely with his own kind.

He had met other foxes during this time but had never formed a friendship. He was too wary, still blighted by his early experiences and treatment and he gave his trust to no one. These two vixens were a new experience, and he could not help himself.

He was mature and big and strong and handsome, even more so, curiously, for the loss of one ear gave him a roguish appearance and he accepted and enjoyed the playful attentions of his female suitors. They would spend days together, huddled in the spacious caverns of a disused badger sett, and they hunted in unison, through the nights and into the new year.

The dark vixen came into season first and Cadno mated with her until her time of passion cooled. Within a few days, her sister craved attention and Cadno, called again to do his duty, co-operated eagerly. The first flurry of January snow saw them still together in their badger sett and that night, as the fall increased, they curtailed their hunting and sought an early refuge in the passages below the ground. They had hardly satisfied their hunger and, the next day, made an early start to find food.

Emerging into the blinding white of a new world, they were mystified by the changed appearance of the land. The river slipped slowly by, hardly daring to move, it seemed, and no living thing disturbed the silence, save for some hungry birds. At first they played boisterously, jumping and racing, but the snow clung coldly to their fur and balled in their feet and their activity increased their hunger.

All they could find that night was a rabbit, caught in a gin trap, and a thin, frozen bird, more feather than food. They had searched and roamed far from their badger sett and, as the night ended, they pushed their way into a smaller sett, scraping the snow from the entrance with their paws and settling down to sleep, in spite of their half-empty bellies.

Tom Flanders hurried about, trying to warm himself. He had pulled on his clothes hastily, after jumping out of bed with a rush, shivering as he saw the ice on the inside of his bedroom window. His ears were stone cold, almost frostbitten, and his nose tingled. As his fire lit, he huddled over it, almost touching the new-born flames as he tried to warm himself. Bruiser slept on, undisturbed.

Tom positioned a metal sheet over the grate to increase the airflow through the fire and soon the flames leapt up the chimney as the cokes burned brightly and the fire roared. Bruiser came out from the bedroom and sat directly in front of the blaze, almost as close to it as Tom, and his owner, smiling, bent to touch the strong black muzzle. Soon they had breakfasted, Tom sitting in a wooden armchair drawn up before the fire while Bruiser lay close to him with his head raised, patiently waiting for scraps to come his way. The man drank a cup of scalding hot, strong tea and, well prepared for the elements, tied a muffler about his throat, donned his heavy coat and woollen gloves, and set off over the fields with a shovel on his shoulder and Bruiser at his heels.

The terrier, if he resented the snow, did not show it. He followed, as usual, in Tom's shadow, ignoring the ground conditions as if he were well used to the cold, crisp, white substance that covered his familiar fields and tracks. The first traps were still in position and Tom thought the weather to be the reason for his lack of success. Few creatures had ventured abroad in the blizzard.

As they passed along the lane where drifts blocked their way and made the passage difficult, Bruiser began to move ahead and soon he was running, almost, in the direction of the small earth. Too late, Tom saw the gaping, opened entrance and realised what the terrier was up to, and he called at him, loudly, but in vain, to try to stop him.

Surprised, a fox will often bolt quickly from his refuge and in the quiet, snow-silent countryside, his cries carried down into the earth and the three foxes immediately sprang into action, rushing through the passages. The two vixens were in front of Cadno and as the first reached the entrance, she slammed straight into the rushing form of Bruiser, knocking him off balance, back in the snow. In spite of the force and the total unexpectedness of the collision, the terrier locked his jaws on to her and would not release his grip, though she struck at him, tearing his snout with her sharp, long fangs.

In one blinding flurry of movement, Cadno and the dark vixen leaped from the earth and sped away over the snow in opposite directions. Tom had immediately noticed the deformed ear of the handsome red fox and realised that Cadno had, once more, crossed Bruiser's path. He smiled, and hoped that the fox would stay in the area, with his new found mate.

Bruiser and the vixen had disappeared from view, deep into a drift, but Tom soon found them. Bruiser's first hold had been at the vixen's right front shoulder and she had been able to twist her head and seize him, burying her curved fangs deep into his muzzle. By his own struggling efforts to free himself and retaliate, the terrier helped to make the wounds worse, but gradually, due to his superior strength and single-minded determination, he was able to change his grip and clamp upon the vulnerable throat of his terrified opponent, who fought for the sheer preservation of her own life. It was soon over then. His powerful jaws shut off the vital air supply and her body shuddered, and became limp and pliant as the mysterious life force, the animal-spirit, left it forever. Her vulpine soul cried silently in the wintry morning and then, destroyed, faded into oblivion and left her earthly body-shell.

Though the vixen had forfeited her life, she had not done so without a desperate struggle, and Bruiser had paid for his valour with a huge, deep gash on the top of his snout. Blood bubbled up from the wound and snorted from his nostrils and Tom cleaned his face with snow, stemming the bleeding as best he could. If the terrier had stayed at his side, they could possibly have accounted for the three foxes, but Tom was not displeased. He had developed an unaccountable admiration for Cadno, and did not grudge him his good fortune.

The snow lasted for three more weeks, hard-packed and frozen by the biting winds, and wild things paid a heavy price. The smaller birds were the first to perish, their spare frames unable to resist the twin evils of numbing cold and gnawing hunger. The lakes froze over, and smaller streams ceased to flow and the bone hard ground, beneath its wintry overcoat, offered no sustenance to the children of the white wastelands. Every day brought further hardship and suffering and soon, even the most timid of animals became more adventurous in their desperation.

Buzzards spoke from the whispering sky and circled high above, searching, keen-eyed, sweeping the land far below for some sign of food. They cried aloud and spread turning wings to catch the wind and soar away and up and on to another range. The crow called with a hoarse and evil voice and had no beauty to plead his case and small animals perished as the cold clasped at them.

During this time, Cadno and his dark bride survived on any scrap, chewing even at frozen swedes and potato peelings at a farm rubbish heap, and a mouldy, half loaf of bread swelled in their bellies and helped to fill them. Soon the ribs showed through the fur on their flanks and their eyes became listless and dull. They had little energy to hunt and slept, close to each other, for long periods below the ground.

Torpid, tough old badgers never stirred from their cosy earth fortresses and lived on their summer-built fat, and their pregnant sows, who often cubbed at Christmas, carried their unborn young to a later birthing and a more kindly climate.

As February approached, old man winter relented and, just in time to save many animals, the thaw set in, stripping the land of its white blanket in a matter of days, and providing access to food for the starving species he had almost eliminated.

In a frenzy of hunting and scurrying and scraping and stealing, the animals of the wild land recovered their strength and reinforced their rundown constitutions. New-found flesh soon clothed their gaunt frames and Cadno built himself again to his handsome litheness, while his dark-coated mate grew fat, not only from food, but from the new lives that developed within her. The miracle of birth was close to her, and wild things knew the heady call of spring.

Cadno felt his spirit soar, and deep within him, hope and elation cheered him. The warm time would soon come and his dark vixen mate had already scraped at a dozen buries, trying and testing and cleaning them for suitability. This one was too spacious for her, and that one, just a little too small, this, too deep, and that, too exposed, and so it went on until, at long last, she was satisfied with an earth on a bracken bank. A small disused badger sett, she scraped open two entrances and inhaled the sweet earth-smell of the tunnels. It had been empty for over four years, since a young boar and sow had been killed there soon after they had occupied it. None of their kind had been near it since, and the entrances had become overgrown and filled with collapsed earth. It was dry and draught free and below, in the wooded valley just one hundred yards away, a bright, fast-flowing stream rushed to join the river. It was ideal.

Cadno, filled with pride, watched her as she left him to go to the birth chamber, and as shadows and shades of evening clothed the sky and the land, he stirred himself from his warm shelter in the bracken. He stretched, he yawned, he scratched diligently at his torn ear, and then he scented the air for some moments before moving away. He was not wanted at the time-for-cubs, and the vixen would not welcome his presence and so he set off, gliding into the night and padding his way effortlessly, gracefully and silently, down the steeply sloping bank. He halted at the bottom to scent mark and relieve himself and then, boldly and brazenly, he marched on and did not stop again until he came to the henhouse at Trealaw, over a mile away. Now he donned the mantle of caution and cunning and stealth and he set about the task of gaining himself a meal.

An agile spring took him almost to the top of the wire mesh run, and he pulled himself up and over, dropping lightly to the other side. A few paces took him to the door, and though the bottom half was bolted firm, the top was open, and he heard the restless hens begin to talk. He sprang again, and balanced himself at the top of the half door, leaning on the unfastened upper part, and opening it wider.

He looked at his prizes, sitting anxious on their perches, unsettled and frightened, and he exulted in his youth and strength and power over them, and he discarded his cloak of caution.

He would rather be a fox than a captive cur.

He had known the constraints of a collar and despised the canine species that subjected themselves to the whims of their capricious masters.

Petted one day, put down, the next, they lived in trust and rolled doleful, simple eyes at their owners.

Cadno knew, full well, his place in the grand scheme of life.

He trusted no one.

He leapt from the top of the door and, in that instant, began his carnage.

The first hen died quickly and, excited by the fear vibrations of his victims, he worked himself into a murderous frenzy, killing, killing, killing until his jaws were stiff and his gums were sore and his mouth and tongue drenched in blood. His cruel madness dominated him and hens surrounded him, lifeless bundles of feathers on the floor and, at last, and suddenly, all was silent. Twenty-three hens were dead, and dust filled the air and odd feathers floated down and Cadno, panting, his tongue lolling from his mouth and blood-flecked slaver on his lips, looked about, well pleased with himself. He bit off the head of a plump bird which lay at his feet and then he picked up a still-twitching victim, and carried her towards the door. He could not jump out, she was too heavy. He tried again, but could not reach the top, and again he tried, but it was no use.

Still holding the hen, he walked around the shed and there, sure enough, he *found* a way out. There was still the fence to negotiate. In the farthest corner, the wire was rusted and perished and he tore at it with his feet and fangs until he was able to squeeze under it, dragging the hen through with him. He started on his way back to the bracken bank.

His vixen would be hungry in the morning, and he would leave her some of his spoils.

Chapter 9

Return to the Valley

Tom Flander's return to the mining valley where he had spent his turbulent years, was not a happy occasion.

The whole country had been shocked by the tragedy of the explosion at his old colliery but, for him, it was of more personal importance. Friends had perished. Old friends. Good friends. And his community, which had once given him love and admiration, was scarred, once more, by the cruel demands of the black diamond.

He mourned the loss with a keen grief, even though he had always believed it better to die quickly, in strength, than to wilt and wither and bow to the heavy years. To him, quality of life was more important than its length, and he rarely mourned for those that passed swiftly, without time for suffering. He reserved his pity for those who called to death as a friend but were forced to patiently wait until it crept upon them, in decay.

But good friends, true friends, had been taken in the full bloom of their life. Widows were left to weep and fatherless children eventually dried their eyes and wondered, and remembered. He had experienced it all before, in the impressionable years of his youth, and he still paid a price, deep in the darkest recesses of his mind. Still dreamed of horses, mules, humans, blown apart to fall in the same mire and lie together in grotesque and sickening death as the rats, and the elements fused them into the same soil. One beginning. One end. From the earth to the earth. Ever would it be the same.

As he walked along the platform, he felt the oppression.

It seemed to descend and settle upon him with a physical

presence, determined to weigh over his shoulders and beat him down. He handed his ticket to the collector and nodded in reply as the man recognised him and greeted him, even after all these years. Why not, he thought? In these hills, sporting heroes never truly died. The platform stood in the shadow of the very hall where he had fought many of his early contests. The spectators could almost touch the fighters and those in the balcony, had they leaned too far, would have fallen over the guardrail and landed in the ring. They had a new idol now, Tommy Farr, who would, later that year, go fifteen epic rounds with the Brown Bomber, Joe Louis, before sixty-thousand spectators in New York's Yankee Stadium, the only contest Tommy lost, in that, the best year of his career.

Leaving the station, he crossed the bridge and walked through the gaslit valley streets. Coal grimed and dirty, they had a gloomy aura which was entirely their own. He passed by the house where the washerwoman lived and glimpsed her in her open shed, where she stood at the steaming wooden tub all day, scrubbing for the well-off, with sleeves rolled up over her brawny arms, taking in washing to provide for her children and her health-ruined husband.

The bone chilling cold and the driven, filthy rain, swept across the glinting, glistening streets where gutters ran with gushing water. He thought it little wonder that the great depression had settled on the valleys just a few years earlier. It had felt at home in such surroundings, and had made it its headquarters. A series of towns, with a pit at the end of almost every street, they said, and tomorrow the people of this valley would bury their dead and long columns of mourners would walk to the cemetery. Tomorrow he would be, once more, a son of this valley, so proud, with so little to be proud of. It was a feature of the coalfield that those who came to live and work among them, quickly became one of them. Accepted, integrated, in a manner which would never come to pass in country life, where a stranger remained a stranger, often for many years.

Today, he had to show his respect and sympathy for one who, during his valley years, had done so much to help him.

In the cruel industry of the time, many mining wives became widows. Special were those who managed it twice. She had given Tom a roof over his head after the war and he, in turn, had helped her to recover from the loss of her first husband. His rent assisted her financially but, perhaps even more importantly, his presence helped her through her despair. A presence, someone to sit quietly beside the fire in the long winter evenings, reading a book. Someone she could glance toward as she darned his socks. Someone she could cook for, wash for, iron for. Someone she could take care of.

He had never made any advances towards her, though she was still an attractive woman, a woman he admired and respected, but instinctively, he knew she was one who needed to mourn, and mourn long until her duty to her mate had been done in full. She never gave Tom any idea of her feelings toward him, kept herself at a distance and somehow they had managed to avoid the desperate temptations and dangers which presented themselves to a young widow and a virile athlete, with a lost legacy of youth to make up.

When Tom went from her life she was ready to take up again the role of the living, loving, mining wife and she had married one of her late husband's best friends, himself left alone when his wife fell to the wasting disease, tuberculosis. Now he, too, had gone, and would lay beside her remains in the cold, wet earth, newly opened to receive him.

Tom walked down the claustrophobic terrace, the narrow cobbled road sandwiched between the steep, pressing hillside and the long row of small houses. It was still so familiar, as if he had never been away. He stopped at the fresh-painted front door, and removed his hat. He did not knock. He lifted the latch and opened the door slowly, and stepped inside, straight into the warm living-room, where a coal fire showed its only merry face among solemn faces, gloomy faces, the faces of the bald-headed men and black-decked woman, who were seated all around the room. He saw, but did not see, for his eyes were drawn immediately to Jane. Her face was swollen and pale and her eyes spoke silently of a great sadness and yet, in her grief, she retained a

The long row of small houses.

dignity and a beauty of character which came from within. He manoeuvred his way around the table, brushing against the legs of the seated mourners in the confined space and, bending toward her, he held her shoulders and kissed her lightly, gently, on each wet cheek. He kissed her eyelids, but she rose from the chair, and clung to him, as a mother to a son, and great sobs convulsed her body.

Jane, Jane, Jane.

It was all he could think of, and he spoke her name repeatedly, nursing her and swaying her as if she were a child, totally in sympathy with her sorrow and yet, somehow erotically stirred by her clean freshness and the solemn control with which she attempted to take hold of her feelings and stop them from overwhelming her.

She had not changed much. Older. Weren't they all? And his presence gave her strength once more and she asserted herself and saw to it that he had a cup of tea and some beef and bread and pickled onions.

The sorrow of the house was the same sorrow of every mining family where the breadwinner lay in his coffin, dressed in his best suit, in the front room. The sorrow when men went to work alive and vital and were brought home dirty, dead, broken and defeated, by the hard rock they worked in. Coalfields claimed their victims and old women washed and prepared them for burial and coal owners' skinny clerks made up the pay and sent it home after the corpse, paid up until the moment life had been lost, perhaps not even to the end of the shift. Inquests would often declare it to be an act of God, and the God they blamed, who moved mysteriously, would weep in His heavens and pour tears upon His children as they lowered their loved ones into His soil.

Later, Tom paid his respects, in the candlelit parlour where the smell of the wooden coffin and heavy scented flowers hung oppressively. Unlike many of his fellow victims, who had been crushed or burned too badly to be displayed, Jane's husband lay, with a wax-like face, and a bland expression.

Tom guessed, correctly, that he had been younger than Jane and could imagine him, lively and handsome, bringing her to life after the self-induced, prolonged, near-death of her cataplectic-like mourning.

He followed through the streets in the company of thousands and he stood bare-headed at the graveside and sang the tragic farewells as only valley miners could, weaned as they were on sorrow, calamity and want. He soaked himself in the emotion of the close-packed mourners as the soaring tenors and the swelling baritone and bass voices washed about him. With the unshakable and characteristic love of his race for the old, moving hymns, he joined in the singing, his body present but his brain absent, away over the hills and fields of time. The expressive harmonies brought him to the verge of tears and more than once he found himself blinking, hard, to control himself. Memories of his life flooded before him, happy times, and sad, triumph and tragedy, and the relentless nostalgia weighed upon him, permeating his very bones and blood and sinew and making him as one with his proud Welshness.

On the Monday, he caught a train, back to Bruiser.

Two months later, he bought a writing pad. He was not much for letter writing and it took him almost a week to draft something suitable, writing, re-writing, making errors, altering. At last he was satisfied, and posted it from the box in the village. He had asked Jane to join him.

He had offered her a home.

He had asked her to share his life.

Within a week, he had a reply.

Politely, as gently as she could manage, she turned him down.

He had not offered love.

Chapter 10

The Family of Foxes

Cadno had been lucky.

His slaughter in the henhouse had coincided with two events which overshadowed his opportunism and forestalled pursuit, and possible punishment. While the fox had been busy wiping out the chickens, Tom had been paying his respects in the valley and Lewis, the huntsman, had taken a bad fall from his horse, a fall which would effectively end his hunting career.

The farmer could do nothing about his loss, other than surround his coops with snares and gin traps at every likely place. It was too little, and too late, and was unsuccessful, for Cadno never returned.

Spring is the youth of the year. The infant of the seasons, as summer is the prime of life and autumn is maturity to winters senility. Spring, like the child, can be forgiven its excesses and is admired for its guileless enthusiasm. Cadno was a father, and though it would be some weeks before he was allowed to see his cubs, he helped his dusky mate to bring them safely through the early time. He hunted and scavenged as never before and was so diligent in his methods that no one ever suspected the presence of the litter in their earth on the bracken bank.

He spent most of his waking hours in providing for himself and his family and he would carry food to the earth, sometimes pushing it down into the entrance, sometimes leaving it close by. Though the cubs took no solid food for the first weeks, their mother's appetite increased as she suckled her hungry brood, whose attentions soon left her teats raw and sore and stripped of their covering of belly fur.

Cadno kept well clear of man, well clear of the lambing fields, even though the scents and sounds were such an attraction. His animal spirit had allowed him one lapse at the henhouse, but now it asserted itself and guided him away from danger. He must protect his cubs and the lovely mother who had given them life. Hardly a day passed when he was unlucky in his search, almost every day he would provide them with something to eat. He caught rabbits and mice and settling river birds and once he had even attacked a cob swan, majestic at the edge of the rushes. Its reaction soon made him realise the error of his ways and he fled, humiliated, before its spitting, snorting, stretching feathered venom. It was another experience, yet another lesson. there was still, it seemed, so much for him to learn.

Before the cubs were allowed to leave their secure earth, the vixen often left them for long periods, coming to Cadno and helping him to hunt, but not roaming too far away. They would spend nights together, searching the nearby wood, pillaging the forest floor, and glorying in each other and in the freedom and beauty of their life. They would return to the earth and Cadno would lay outside as she went in to tend to their children. They wanted meat now, for her milk no longer satisfied them and soon they devoured her meal offerings with ever increasing ferocity, quarrelling and fighting and ripping at the small carcasses placed before them. They had shared their first solid food, regurgitated by the vixen, in an orderly fashion, but when a rabbit or feathered victim was brought to them, it was always the strongest that fed best. Seven cubs, Five vixens and two dogs, all healthy and strong and vigorous.

Cadno was allowed to see them at last, to mix among them.

How he enjoyed it.

He played with them as if he himself were a cub and allowed them to tug at his handsome brush and shake at his throat. He never punished them or harmed them in any way, even when they became over active and extreme in their roughness. He was proud of them and soon they were all hunting together and though the cubs were not yet stealthy, and ruined many a stalk by their clumsiness, Cadno would not be angry, for he had never been more content.

They were growing, and soon they would have to be moved to another earth. Beside the stench which their presence had caused, their movement and play around the entrance holes had flattened the bracken and gave evidence of their occupation which could be seen at some distance. She knew where she would take them, and the mother spent a day and half a night there, opening out the new quarters and making it suitable for their occupation, after first satisfying herself that it was completely safe. There had been no disturbance since she had last visited it. There were no tell-tale signs, or scents.

That morning, she left Cadno down at the stream, and carried a well-grown rabbit back to the bury to feed the cubs, Cadno stood in the reeds and watched her go. How daintily she picked her way across the dew-covered fields. How carefully she concealed herself, making use of every natural shield and shade. He saw her pause, shaking the wetness from her coat, before she entered the old birth chamber. He *thought* he saw a small muzzle push out to greet her, but perhaps it was only his imagination. He knew his children would be eager for their meal, eager to snatch the rabbit from her. Her haunches and her dark brush disappeared into the earth and Cadno settled down. How lucky he was to have such a family.

He could not know that he would never see her, or the cubs, again.

* * * * *

Tom Flanders was self-sufficient.

He had paid for his cottage with money put aside from his ring earnings and this had still left him with a little capital to live off. He supplemented this in many ways. There was always plenty of scope for a willing worker in the country, and he had no difficulty in finding jobs, for his services were in such demand that he could not always cope with all the requests that came his way. He worked for long spells at the mansion, as a handyman, in the stables, with the gardeners, with the gamekeepers. He helped at hay making, he helped at shearing, he shepherded the lambing flocks. Now he was also called to assist the new huntsman. Gareth had taken over, inheriting the pack from his father, whose advice would prove to be invaluable, but he could no longer be of practical assistance to his son, who had many ideas about improving the pack. Tom gave him his time whenever it was needed. Care of the lambing flocks, and care of the hounds, complemented each other. Combined with his ownership of good working terriers, he was always very busy when cubs were born to vixens, and ewes brought forth their harvest of lambs.

Vixens and their cubs were killed whenever possible.

It was a job that Tom did not relish, but he accepted it as essential, destroying the vixen and her family as humanely as he could. Now he had found a way to avoid the worst of it, and earn some money at the same time. Rather than destroy them, he would, whenever possible, take them alive. He had a ready market for them. Hunts paid well when their country was short of foxes, and soon Tom had established good contacts, sending vixens and their cubs to the nearer parts of England.

There would never be a shortage in his native hills. No matter how many foxes were disposed of, there was never any scarcity. Season after season, they thrived, and Tom marvelled at their ability to resist such losses. Where did they all come from?

At home in his outbuildings, he had two litters ready for despatch. To fine vixens, and a total of eleven strong cubs. The master of the Romilly foxhounds had arranged their collection later in the week, and Tom decided that another litter would make his three hundred mile round trip, more worthwhile. He knew they would be given every opportunity to thrive in the Romilly country until they matured, to replenish their native foxes, many of which had succumbed to the scourge of mange, and had to be ruthlessly culled.

* * * * *

Cadno was restless, the day would be too warm. Already, flies buzzed about him and annoyed him. He moved twice to find peace, but it was no use. Wherever he went, they pursued him and now, to make matters worse, magpies had found him and were beginning to persecute him. How he would like to close his jaws on their throats! But they were far too clever, far too cautious. They knew how to be a nuisance without putting themselves in any danger.

Reluctantly, with his contented mood of the early morning rapidly vanishing, he wandered over to a three-hole earth, half a mile from his family, and settled down in the cool darkness, to spend a lazy day.

* * * * *

With two sacks, and a spade over his shoulder, a terrier running at his heels, Tom crossed the fields towards the bracken bank, with its revealing bare patches. Since the vixen and her brood had been in occupation, they had opened a total of five entrances. To a countryman, to a foxhunter, they beckoned alluringly and told a tale as old as the hills themselves.

Bruiser had been left at home.

He was useless for this job.

Cubs had no chance. Indeed, very often, their dam had no chance.

Bruiser was not wanted for an expedition such as this. The terrier which now danced in front of Tom was a small bitch. She was a sure marker and would bay steadily. She would drive her opponents to a stop end and keep them occupied without harming them too much. For this job, Sally was invaluable.

She was ahead of Tom now, her pace had quickened.

She was making for the old, three-holed earth. Tom had never had a fox from it, but he hurried to follow and saw her push into an entrance. He did not want to see a vixen bolt out, abandoning her cubs.

* * * * *

Inside, Cadno was instantly on guard. His nostrils told him of the danger and his ears, flattened to his head, confirmed the message.

He had an unwelcome visitor.

Sally crept warily down, deeper into the earth.

Cadno hurled himself towards the bitch.

Completely surprising her.

He slammed into her and clamped his strong jaws over her muzzle.

She cold not retaliate, for her held her firm, and continued his momentum, forcing her backwards. The little terrier struggled and squirmed, but she was helpless before him. The huge fangs had pierced just in front of her eyes, and the under jaws of the fox, in its pincer movement, drove the lower fangs into the soft space beneath the terrier's mouth. Tom, kneeling at the entrance, heard the terrier's cries of pain and then saw Sally retreating towards him, a sight he had never before witnessed. She was being driven backwards, bundled out of the earth and, had it not been for the overwhelming scent of the angry vulpine, he would have expected to see the striped head of a badger but then, as the length of the bitch emerged, and he saw the great head, topped by the mutilated ear, clamping fast to his terrier, he acknowledged, once again, his old antagonist, and he understood.

He cursed himself then, for not having brought Bruiser with him, and he reached over the bitch to try and get a grip on Cadno's head. It was not an easy matter in the confined space, a turmoil of writhing hair and fur, and the lively, blazing yellow eyes saw the groping hand and, realising the danger, loosed the terrier and lunged, in one movement, driving teeth into a new hold on the fleshy ball of the hunter's exposed thumb.

Sally, freed, drove in for Cadno's throat and the fox retreated away from the maddened, furious bitch who now pursued him, reversing their earlier roles. He struck at her in his hasty flight and, with incredible agility, turned and fled down the tunnels, towards the flow of fresh air. He hustled out and galloped away and then, from a matter of thirty yards, he turned and looked at Tom, staring with bold assurance. Sally was out, searching, and Cadno turned again and trotted away.

Tom's hand had been lacerated in the brief confrontation and raw, bloodied flesh bulged from the jagged wound which the fox had ripped open. He took out a large, coloured handkerchief and pressed the torn flesh together, binding it as best he could, with his left hand, conscious of an excruciating pain which throbbed, and travelled up to his wrist, his forearm, his elbow. Sally, searching about, seemed unconcerned by her injuries for her adrenaline was pumping and she was ready for more action. Tom took her to the stream and washed her face and then, removing the handkerchief, he plunged his hand into the cold water, wincing at the stinging pain but cleansing the wound as he did so, watching the crimson stain as it was born away. Already, his hand had started to swell and, not for the first time in his life, he marvelled at the quiet courage and gameness of the small terriers which forced their way below ground to meet with, and overcome, such fury. He wrapped the handkerchief about his hand once more, and used his knife to hack away a sleeve of his shirt, using the torn cloth to bind his wound more securely.

The little bitch was calmer, more settled, and sniffing at the water's edge, lapping in the stream and then rubbing her muzzle with her paw. Picking up his shovel and sacks, he resumed his journey towards the bare-trodden holes on the bracken bank. As he neared them, he tethered Sally and fastened her to a tree before quietly and quickly sealing all the entrances with earth, to block off all possible escape.

* * * * *

So Cadno was a father!

He must be. It was surely no coincidence that he had been laid up so near to the breeding earth. Well, if the cubs were anything like their father, the master of the Romilly would be a very fortunate man. In the seconds when he and Cadno had watched each other, Tom had forgotten his pain. He could not help but admire, again, the spirit and the sheer physical beauty of the fiend-fox which had shown such courage. Tom was tempted to leave the cubs, but he knew it was his duty to get rid of them. If it became known that he had allowed them to go free, he would lose a lot of friends and besides, perhaps Cadno had already sired others, and he lived to sire more and fight on. With all his heart, Tom now wished for just one thing. He wished for Cadno's safety.

He wished him safety from all hazards.

Until.

Until the day when he would go to ground before Bruiser. Then, and only then, would Tom wish harm to befall this magnificent beast, with the form of a fox and the supreme courage of a lion.

* * * * *

When he was certain that all possible bolt holes were blocked, Tom was satisfied. He hated to see a nursing vixen bolt from a bury, forced to flee from her cubs, and when this happened he would, when possible, leave the litter undisturbed, so that the mother could later reclaim them and move them to another refuge.

Vixens were good mothers, brave and caring and would even forfeit their lives for their cubs' protection and Tom would wonder at the thoughts in such an animal's mind if she was forced to abandon her family. He was told that they could not think, could not reason, but surely they were able to feel some sorrow and anguish? They could register love, and birth brought its own, special, possessive love to a mother, so what emotions tore at her if she was forced to place her own safety above that of her litter.

He would take the cubs and think nothing of it, but only if the mother could also be made captive.

He opened an entrance and held Sally for a moment to steady her. Already her face was beginning to swell and her muzzle was tender and sore, even to his gentle touch. She moved in, to search for her adversary.

The dark vixen had known of the danger.

She knew that the earth had been sealed. If she had been alone, she may have bolted, making an escape while she had a chance, but there were her cubs to consider. She still had been tempted to leave them, for self-preservation is a basic and powerful instinct but, while she dithered, the course of events had been decided for her. She was trapped. Tom had closed every possible retreat.

She herded her apprehensive youngsters to the farthest part of the sett, and placed herself, protectively, before them.

Sally worked calmly, methodically, through the tunnels, which were full of scent. The stench of fox and rotting meat combined to nauseating levels, but it did not bother Sally. She had a job to do and, disregarding hardship or danger or the stinging pain which throbbed at her foreface, she would do it. Nothing on earth could stop her. It was as if she was programmed, directed by a superior, irresistible force, to seek out the species which she regarded as her enemy. She would not disturb a badger, had never once worked one, but, if a fox were present, she would bypass any badger that obstructed her route to the quarry. If ever she left an earth, after searching through it, Tom could safely declare it to be unoccupied by a fox. She had never been shown to be wrong.

The tunnels were tight in places but, for most of their length, she was able to manoeuvre comfortably and quickly. She soon found the vixen and her cubs. They were crouched, huddled together, and the cubs were petrified. Their mother, forming a barrier, lay before them, her mouth parted wide, ready for the intruder.

Sally started to bay.

She bayed loudly and savagely, darting towards the vixen and striking occasionally, like a viper, at the form before her. Like fencers, they parried, thrust and parried again and the vixen was forced back, tightly, against her little family. The terrier settled down, baying steadily, mere inches from the potentially punishing jaws of the fox.

Tom soon found her.

It was a shallow spot, some two feet deep, and the noise from the bitch was easily traced. He could feel the grounds vibrations as she tested her opponent. Though his hand was extremely painful and his arm had stiffened, he soon opened out a hole to his terrier and, as he did so, Sally hurled herself at the vixen and

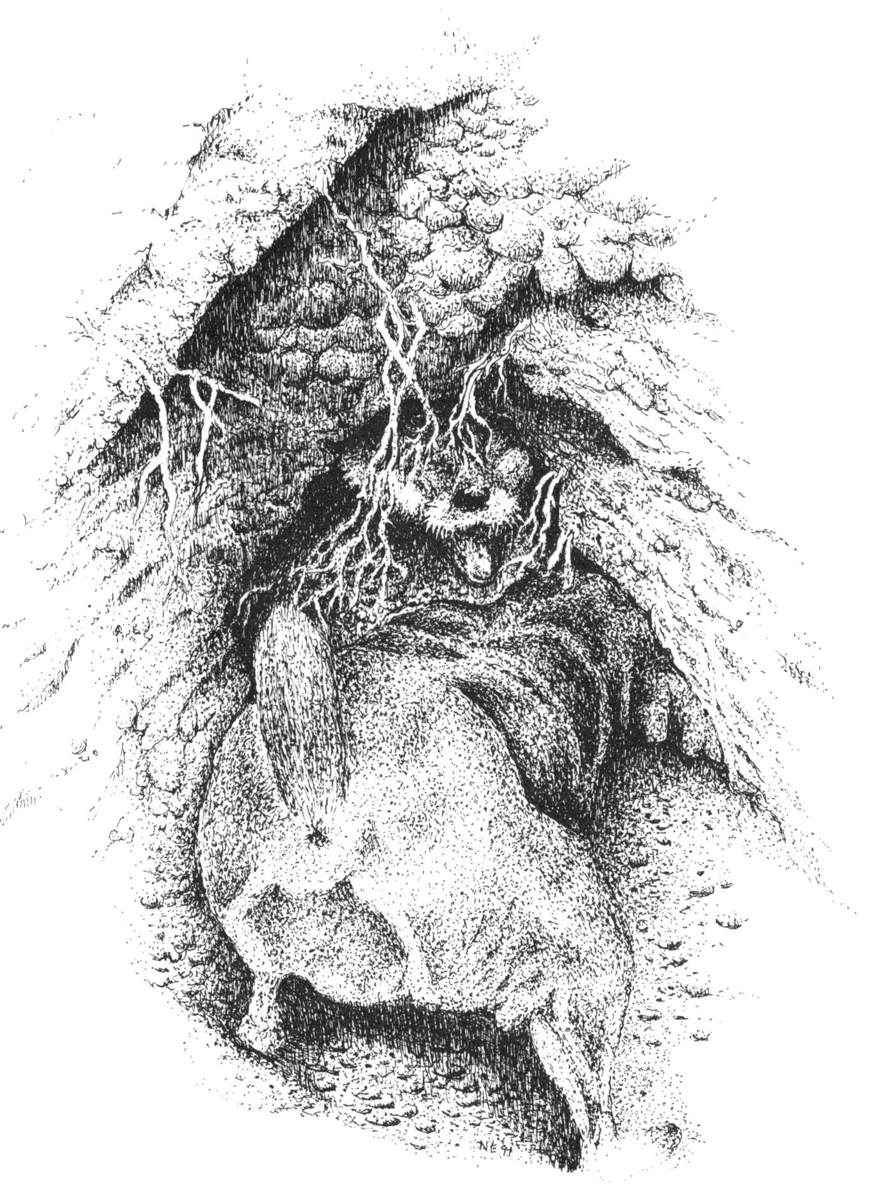

Mere inches from the vixen.

took hold of her at the cheek. In her desperation, the vixen voided her body waste and, jaws agape, the eyes became lifeless and the body limp. For the second time that day, Tom grasped for a fox but this time he was able to easily hold it, and quickly placed it in a sack, freeing the bitch, who returned to the tunnel. Tom knotted a rope around the sack and placed it alongside him on the ground. There was no movement and those ignorant of the ways of the fox might suspect that she had expired, but he knew that no lasting harm had been done to the vixen. She was simply suffering from the shock, the trauma of her captivity and would soon recover. Sally had seized one of the cubs and mouthed the lifeless body as the rest of the litter cowered together. Tom soon bagged them and, as the bitch sniffed at the sacks, he replaced the soil, burying the dead cub and tidying the earth, leaving it almost without trace of the drama that had taken place there.

The vixen stirred in her sack and tried to chew at it but when Tom slung it over his shoulder, she lay motionless once more, hardly stirring.

The van from the Romilly was waiting when Tom arrived home. He made his visitors welcome and, after they had helped him to clean and properly bandage his hand, he tended to Sally and then provided a meal for the men for he knew they had travelled long and would be ready to eat.

They talked of hounds and hunting and foxes, yarning and swapping tales of each pack's exploits but soon it was time for them to start on their return journey, and they loaded their new fox population into the boxes, specially prepared in the van. Each crate contained a good measure of fresh straw and a strong mesh door and each vixen, with her cubs, seemed quite at ease when transferred from Tom's custody. Three healthy vixens, seventeen good cubs. It would be a welcome addition to their territory and the master would be well pleased. They counted the notes into Tom's hand, and still thanking him, took their leave.

* * * * *

That evening, Cadno returned, cautiously, to the sett on the bracken bank.

He did not need to enter its passages. The scent told him the whole story. The horrifying scent of the terrier bitch, the vile stench of man.

His lovely, dark vixen had gone, he knew not where, and the cubs were no more.

Was there no end to this devilry, this persecution?

Was there no limit to their pursuit of him, and his kind?

With heavy heart and a step that had lost it spring, he turned away from that happy nursery home and walked slowly across the slope to seek, once more, a new meaning for his life, a life that had, in an instant, returned to its former solitary, and lonely state.

Chapter 11

Something to Celebrate

There had been special celebrations at the mansion.

For more than a week, guests had arrived and departed to take part in the events which had been organised to mark the coming of age of Sir Edwin Lucas' daughter, the rebellious and unconventional Catherine Reid Lucas.

There had been dinners and a glittering ball and handsome young men had sought her out and competed for her attentions. There were peers of the realm and army officers and members of the remnants of the local squirey, and the very best of the county's society. There was even a princess from a remote and minor branch of European run-down royalty, and the staff of the great house worked hard and long, though extra help had been engaged. Even when only Sir Edwin and his wife, Lady Madeline were in residence it seemed to require a host of toiling men and women to ensure the smooth running of their lives. There was a head gardener and four under-gardeners to tend the four acres of garden, providing fresh fruit and vegetables all the year round. A bevy of servants saw to it that they dined each and every day on fresh chicken and only the breast would be eaten, the rest wasted. There were stable staff and gamekeepers and labourers beside all those who worked in the house itself, but they found Sir Edwin to be fair and honest in his dealings though he was a disciplinarian who could be stubborn and hard when the mood suited him.

Tom's services were often required and he was held in high regard by Sir Edwin after he had been able to condition a valuable hunter, bringing it to peak fitness when it had seemed to wilt under the attentions of his experienced stable staff. During these times, the young Catherine was never far from Tom and, to the despair of her mother, spent far too much time in his company. Though she was much younger than Tom, she found him disturbingly attractive and preferred his company to that of the over-attentive, fawning young men from her own background.

She could not be described as a beauty and was not over-endowed with feminine charm, but there was about her, an animal vitality and a nubile bloom which, when he considered it, disturbed Tom.

He had never been what it was fashionable to describe as a "ladies man". For a brief period at the end of the war, he had used a girl or two in the rollicking Rhondda of new-found peacetime, but when he began his career as a fighter, he put all that behind him. When his early, enforced retirement brought his life to the brink of catastrophe, he had many times opened his eyes at dawn in a strange bedroom but, for him, the opposite sex had rarely made him think in terms of a lengthy commitment, and now that he had built for himself a quiet, country life, he would make sure that this potentially menacing temptation did not spoil it. He was careful to treat her in an almost fatherly fashion and told himself that her interest was directed more at his ability with horses than in himself as a man. Anything else would be unthinkable.

Tom lived a mile from the little village, with its small courtroom where poachers were punished and drunkards degraded before the unforgiving magistrates and the tut-tutting, God-fearing deacons. He let an ordered, predictable life and did no work on a Sunday. It was his special day, a day when he attended the grey, stone built chapel and touched his cap to Sir Edwin as he took his stylish wife to the English church, a castle-like structure built, Tom thought, in a style which would remind the Welsh to be servile. As he came out from the service, he was given a message that the hounds would meet at the mansion the following day. A lamb-killer had been at work.

The season had just ended really, and there had been little activity since the last meet. Lambs had not been unduly disturbed, and Tom was glad of it. When killing began, it usually meant that a litter of cubs would need to be destroyed somewhere. And why meet at the mansion? There were no sheep in the area. Tom guessed it to be a further extension of the birthday celebrations and when he arrived the next morning, he was not surprised to see a good field, ready to follow the hounds' progress.

The day was cold and damp and the atmosphere was one of excitement and anticipation. At Benlan farm, a mile away, seven lambs had been lost, a blow no farmer could tolerate, and a start was made with little delay. The latest killing had occurred that very morning and, if the scent held, the culprit could be accounted for.

When they arrived at the place of the death, the hounds went quickly to work and soon, they pushed along the mountainside, following the drag to a deep earth, where they marked strongly. As the hounds and followers cleared the area, Tom entered a young terrier and soon began to dig to the sound of the baying. It was an uneventful dig and not particularly difficult and, when it was completed, a good sized barren vixen was accounted for.

Fastening the terrier to a tree, Tom began to backfill the site when he became aware of the approach of one of Sir Edwin's guests, a young army officer, Captain Ridley, who showed an interest in the black terrier, sitting placidly at his tether, his work completed, his face peppered with minor wounds.

"I've heard a great deal about these terriers of your Flanders, is he for sale?"

"Oh no sir, I never sell them" replied Tom, "just keep them for my own use sir." Respectful, Correct.

"Oh come now, you'll hardly miss one I'm sure. Will a fiver buy him?"

This was becoming difficult.

Sir Edwin was smiling, talking to the captain. "What would you do with a terrier Ridley? These are workers, not show dogs. Can't take these to Crufts."

"Five pounds. Here now. I'll not take no for an answer", and the captain threw the note in front of Tom, walking across to the terrier, taking out a knife as he did so. Too late, Tom realised that the captain did not intend to cut the tether and, in an instant, he held the dog's head firmly and, quickly and savagely, cut across its throat with the sharp blade.

The small terrier fell to the turf, its life blood draining away.

"There, he'll kill no more foxes. We want sport not slaughter. Dead foxes don't run." He was smiling, pleased with himself.

A murmur of disgust came from the followers and Sir Edwin looked on, obviously shocked.

Tom picked up the five pound note and walked over to the captain, slowly, menacingly, but none were prepared for what was to follow.

"I'll not be needing this sir", he said, and pushed the money in to a pocket of the officer's tunic. "I'll take my payment this way." And he hammered two short left hooks to the unprotected belly. The air was driven from the soldier's lungs and his mouth sagged open as Tom switched another crushing blow to the slack jaw. He felt the bone crack as he connected and he heard the scream of agony with satisfaction and saw the face begin to swell, even before the man hit the ground. He saw the eyes glaze, like those of a dead fish and the mouth gaped and gasped as the stomach retched with the muscle-tearing strain. A glorious pain swept up Tom's forearm. It was a jarring, hammer-blow of satisfaction and a tidal wave of relief, eased his pent-up tension.

It all happened so quickly. As startled men rushed to tend to the army officer, Tom picked up the dead terrier and buried him with the vixen. He collected his tools and walked away, and his step was proud and his bearing dignified. Tears washed his cheeks, and he did not want to be seen. He had used his fists in anger for the first time for many years. He had prided himself on his self-control, but a man could take only so much. His bible told him to turn the other cheek. Forgive. He tried to live according to its teachings, but there was also a passage that permitted an eye for an eye. He could not let such an act of callous cruelty go unpunished. He had just stood there and witnessed the murder of the first son of Bruiser.

Lost him to the act of a barbarian.

He could not help but react.

The punch had carried all his hatred and would expunge, forever, some deeply buried resentments. He had passed it all on to the class who had ordered his comrades to senseless death in the trenches. Wrought some revenge for the poverty and privatation of the valley people when coal owners had cut their wages and starved them, in reluctant, truculent obedience, back to work.

It had felt so good.

He did not know what the consequences would be and, at that moment, he did not care.

He could always go back to the valleys.

Before he reached his cottage, he was calmer. He had regained his composure. In spite of the loss of the young terrier, he could even manage a smile.

He did not realise it, but he had exorcised some deep-seated personal devils from his subconscious.

He had also, surely, brought an end to their celebrations.

Chapter 12

Shoulders a Burden

Over the mountain, in a one-hole earth with the entrance hidden under an overhanging rock, a little vixen tended her first litter.

It was difficult for her.

He mate had not helped he in any way.

She had seen him last, when she entered the birth chamber and had no way of knowing that his body was now suspended on a gamekeeper's gibbet, surrounded by dozens of corpses, fur and feathered. While she had been *giving* life beneath the ground, her partner had been intent on *taking* life at the enclosure where the gamekeeper watched over his prized bantams. As one would expect from such a man whose waking hours were dedicated to the safety of his feathered charges, his hens were well protected and when the steel jaws of a gin trap closed about his leg, the fox eventually welcomed death as a merciful release from the excruciating pain which sent waves of nausea coursing through his body, as the cruel, relentless pressure drove the metal fangs deep into his muscle, his flesh, his very bone. In future years, the traps would be made illegal and men who now used them without a second thought, would come to regard them as the instruments of torture they undoubtedly were.

The little vixen suckled her five blind new-born cubs and spared no effort in her devotion to her brood. She quickly lost condition, when the ever-demanding mouths sought increasing portions of food, and her own appetite was suppressed, as she did her best to sustain them.

As she hunted along the reedy banks of the river, she met Cadno, and a tentative friendship developed. Soon he was carrying carcasses to the entrance of her hideout and when the cubs eventually left the nursery, to appear outside, warily peeping from under the rock, Cadno watched them from a distance with a pride little less than he would have felt for his own, so recently lost.

As the cub's appetites increased, Cadno and his new vixen busied themselves every night, hunting diligently while the cubs waited at the earth. Soon they would be able to accompany their mother but it was, as yet, too early to begin their education.

The two foxes set out as soon as it was dark. Cadno stopped in the marshy field and stood motionless, one leg raised. Soon, he pounced, like a cat, and two long, webbed legs hung from his mouth. He threw the frog into the air and caught it deftly, tossing it high once more, then he tore it in two and leapt on another. There were frogs everywhere and he buried one in a small hole, covering it with a piece of turf. Only two webbed feed could be seen and he scratched more earth, with his paws, covering them completely. He tired of his game and searched after the vixen, but she was not to be seen and soon he fed on mice and voles and drew earthworms from their safety in the soil. When he had fed, he set out determinedly to find the vixen.

He sensed her presence.

He recognised her scent.

He barked.

There was no answer.

He moved slowly, cautiously, along the hedge, and he barked again, calling to her.

In the far distance, a farm dog yapped, faintly, but it was not the reply that he sought. He padded across the field in a half circle, regaining the hedge a hundred yards away and again he called to her.

Something was wrong.

Something had happened to her.

Keeping as close to the hedge as he could, moving deliberately, quietly, stealthily, he was drawn, irresistibly along.

Then he stopped.

He would go no further.

There was an ominous silence.

An aura of calamity.

The spirit of death, which he knew so well, was again abroad.

He backed away and barked.

He turned, and trotted to the corner of the field and he called, anxiously, in their special language.

He knew there would be no reply.

The moon crossed the heavens and bathed the sleepy fields with its pale rays and Cadno, restless, called and barked and retraced his steps but no one took heed and nothing answered him, for even the farm dog had grown tired of the game and slept soundly in his kennel, secured to his chain.

The shy hare loped along and listened briefly, and badgers trod their ancient paths, uncaring, in their own little world and under the rock, the cubs were hungry and ventured out and watched the dawn and waited in vain for their mother. As the birds prepared for another day, Cadno came silently to the cubs and dropped a fat rabbit for them, tearing at the stomach, opening it, for their teeth were not yet strong. They fought over it with real ferocity and covered themselves with its gore as they ripped and tore at it, and when they had finished, they returned to their cavern under the stone and settled down to wait for the dam they did not know they had lost.

Cadno rested in a pile of timber at the bottom of the hill and he slept fitfully, awake at every slight disturbance and ready for flight. He did not wait for night but set out even before the sun had settled and he caught the first early rabbit with a rush and a pounce and a snap. He did not eat any of it though he was, once more, ready for a meal, but he carried it to the rock and dropped it at the entrance for the cubs to feed upon.

When it was dark, he returned to the hedge and quartered the fields in the near vicinity. He called incessantly and his voice carried in the still, warm air. The cry was passed from tree to tree and along the hedgerows and over the fields and far away, a terrier growled in his sleep, and his hackles stiffened. Bruiser opened his eyes and turned over, listening for a while, then he settled himself comfortably, closed his eyes, and applied himself, once more, to the serious business of sleep.

Cadno had searched in every direction, yet he had not returned to the place where the spirit of death still lingered. He approached, once more, the fateful hedge and forced himself to walk its length. The fearful presence was strong but still he walked, slowly on and then, at last, he saw the well worn grass, the parted branches, the passage, the gap in the hedge where countless fox feet had trod. He knew now what had happened and his fear vibrations told him that the snare had been reset and waited, ever vigilant, for the next victim. His nostrils recognised the last mortal scent of the vixen he had met so recently and he knew that their paths would never cross again on this earthly plane. It was his duty to ensure the survival and education of the litter she had left behind. Somehow, across the void where he could not yet follow, her abstract shadow fell over him and he was entrusted with the duties she was now unable to perform.

There was no time to lose.

* * * * *

As he returned to the earth below the rock, he tore at the flesh of a still-born lamb and carried the rear half back to the cubs.

They were grateful for the meal, ever hungry, and fought over it even as Cadno, without ceremony, left them to it, disappearing from sight before they had finished the squabbling and the fighting. He had a job to do. He must find them a new home and teach them the life of a fox.

By mid-day, he had located an earth just half a mile from the birthplace. It was roomy, but not too big. An old rabbit warren which badgers had enlarged though rarely used, it would be ideal for the fast-growing cubs. Cadno curled up in its farthest corner and slept away the rest of the day.

He slept soundly, and when he ventured out he found that night had already fallen. He made straight for the cubs and, as if well used to the procedure, led them to their new home. When they were safely installed below the ground, he set about finding their evening meal, but it was not an easy matter and he hunted for half the night before he was successful, returning to the earth with a very small rabbit. As he came to the new home, he found the cubs outside, already enjoying a meal, under the watchful eyes of an old grey vixen. Here was good fortune indeed, and as Cadno approached, the old matriarch prostrated herself before him in an attitude of submission, writhing and gaping. The cubs seized his offering and he sniffed at the wizened vixen, scent marking and acting as though he were unconcerned for her assistance. Where had she come from? It is a remarkable fact that orphaned cubs are sometimes reared by barren vixens who willingly accept responsibility for the youngsters, adopting them and rearing them as their own. It is not unusual, even, for more than one vixen to take over these duties, but for now, Cadno was content to let this newcomer take the burden from his young and inexperienced shoulders. They would be in better care than he could offer and he could resume his life, the life of the wandering dog fox, going where he would and doing as he wished.

He stayed near the earth for almost a week and during that time he helped feed the cubs, watching over them as they followed their new mother and began to learn the art of fox-living.

He spend the remainder of the summer roving woodland and forest and field, searching the mountains and the valleys. He learned of his territory and its inhabitants. He saw his kind killed in trap and snare. He saw them shot at and chased by dogs of all types. He sheltered under Rhododendron bushes, alive with colour and he kept on the move, restless, cautious, learning, ever learning. He took time to rest under summer hedgerows, alive to the constant hum of countless insects, enjoying the sweet scent. He listened to the bubbling cry of the curlew and saw the distressed display of the startled lapwing, rising in fear from the meadow, to hastily conceal the whereabouts of her young ones, performing her drunken aerobatics in the early summer sky.

He watched and saw the magpie, omen of doom, the black and white pirate, as it pillaged and wreaked havoc among the song bird nestlings, using its cruel, cutlass-heavy beak to slaughter them in their cradle, despite the fluttering protests of the parents.

On they went, into the open farm buildings, to seek out the downy home of the russet-throated swallows and hurl the young, broken, to the floor, staining wicked black beaks in the lifeblood of their helpless victims and laughing, raucously.

He moved through tall-stalked foxgloves, in purple glory, defenceless against the myriad plundering bees, and he cached his surplus morsels under hawthorn bushes and blackthorn in snow-blossomed splendour but, all too soon, the summer of plenty passed and as the days grew shorter and the evenings cooler, he found his territory to be less populated than in early spring. Many cubs had not even completed their first six months of life. Gin traps took a heavy toll and brought death too horrible, too painful, for any animal to deserve, but those that survived had gained caution, and wisdom, and were aware that their lives depended upon eternal vigilance.

And hounds came from their kennel once again. And they had a new huntsman. Young and keen and determined to succeed. Gareth brought vitality and a new life to the old pack and the hounds stepped out expectantly. Long months lay ahead. Foxes would escape or die. There were no half measures.

Life, or death.

It would depend on skill and fitness.

It would depend on courage and guile.

It would depend on luck.

If the fox-spirit smiled and watched with sympathy, perhaps the hounds would be foiled.

But many would die as the fox-spirit frowned, and turned to look the other way.

Chapter 13

Another Season

The room, so warm and welcome in winter, when reflected flames from the fire danced and flickered over the brasses, seemed, somehow, dingy and oppressive in the heat of the summer. It was as if it withdrew, defensively, before the bright sunlight, unable to compete, feeling itself to be drab and unworthy. Tom relied on a fire of peat during the summer months, saving the luxury of coal for the winter. He had grown accustomed to the brightness and heat of a coal fire when he worked in the valley towns and he treated himself, indulged himself, with its warmth and company during the long, cold evenings. Others spent their money at the inn. Tom preferred the warmth and coziness and comfort of the armchair in front of the blazing grate, sitting, thinking, planning, remembering, as the fire crackled, the kettle hissed, and the old grandfather clock ticked the mellow seconds of his life away.

The incident with Captain Ridley had passed into village history and would be retold many times to successive generations.

When Sir Edwin had called at the cottage in the spinney, Tom was prepared for the worst, but he was unrepentant. He could have faced prosecution and, at the very least, expected to be told that his services would no longer be required at the mansion and the kennels, but he was pleasantly surprised when the powerful Sir Edwin had offered, not censure, but sympathy.

The captain had returned to his regiment with a broken jaw, and his face would forever bear a lopsided appearance. He went away with a better understanding of the importance of the hunt in remote Wales where sport, though highly regarded, took second place to the essential control of the fox. He would never be seen again at the mansion and the two men, the pugilist and the peer, drank a whisky and sat together and talked the evening away and, when they parted, they did so with a mutual respect for each others problems and position in life. Tom, perhaps for the first time, began to realise and accept that possession of wealth and power did not automatically mean that humanity would be absent. His years as a collier, his experiences of coal-owner treachery and working class deprivation, had so clouded his outlook that he had gone through life with an outsize mistrust of everyone in a position of authority but now, with the friendship of the fair-minded country estate owner, his attitude began to expand and mature.

He had spent a great deal of time that summer, helping the new huntsman at the kennels. They had rebuilt the more dilapidated parts of the crumbling hound lodges and had added a secure new exercise yard and repaired the walls and railings, sawing, hammering and painting until the kennels were hardly recognisable, so great was the improvement. There were young hounds, eager to enter, ready to begin their working lives and there were younger puppies, bred from the best of the old bitches. Dana and Ruby had tended to litters and, for both these hounds, the puppies were to be the last they would raise. Their last matings to carry on the old lines.

Tom had used Bruiser to sire a litter, mating him to a grand little red working bitch, and he watched the progeny grow and gave them plenty of attention from their early days, when they squeaked like lapwings, through their first weeks, until their legs were steady. Bruiser was every inch the worker. His temperament was superb and his puppies took the most blatant liberties with him, even taking a bone from his mouth as he lay gnawing at it during the long, lazy days. They pulled at his ears and fastened on the tight muscles of his rear legs and they crawled all over him as he tried to find peace, and shelter from the sun.

Even when his muzzle was sore with fresh working wounds, he never lost his temper with them and the nearest they came to retribution was a threatening snarl and a curl of the lip. Not so with their mother. She punished their every misdemeanor and made it plain that her will had to be obeyed.

Bruiser had worked an otter than summer, though Tom had not encouraged him. A visiting pack of otter hounds had marked at a holt on a bed in the river and when Tom was asked to try Bruiser, he entered the terrier, and the dog had needed little encouragement. It was quick, and uneventful and the otter soon bolted, losing the hounds in a stretch of deep water a mile down the river.

Bruiser was kept as a fox dog for Tom rarely used him to the badger. After his first encounter with Brock when he had been virtually unmarked, Bruiser developed a habit of working too recklessly and on more than one occasion he had been punished unmercifully by the powerful jaws of the badger, jaws which had, over the years, ruined many an otherwise good, working terrier. Given time, Bruiser would settle to the task, working properly, but Tom preferred to keep him away from the huge badger setts for now, concentrating, instead, on control of the fox, the job he did so well.

Summer, for Bruiser, was a time of rest and recuperation, a time when he could let his old wounds heal and recharge his mental batteries. He hunted for rats and killed them by the dozen, treating them with contempt, almost , as an adversary hardly worth his attention, but they served the purpose for which they were intended, restoring confidence which could become jaded, tuning him to a high level of fitness and agility, ready for the restart of his real work.

His first job that season, came from the pheasant shoot. The keeper, on his rounds in the early evening, had shot at a fox which had ventured too near the birds and, though he had missed, the fox had been so startled that he had taken immediate refuge in a small earth close by. The keeper had blocked off the entrances and sent for Tom and though a young terrier was given the first opportunity, it showed little interest and the task fell to Bruiser. Tom had been mildly surprised for he expected the youngster to take to work at the first opportunity, but he did not worry about it. Terriers varied in their attitude and some began work much earlier than others. There would be plenty of time, plenty of chances, as the season progressed.

It took about two hours to account for the fox. The small earth was more extensive than it appeared and when Bruiser was eventually traced, he was hard at work, baying well, about four feet below the surface, directly beneath a large rhododendron bush. The dig was difficult, through stone and roots and the fox was holding the terrier at a raised cavity, behind thick roots. There was no escape and when the terrier was taken from the digging, the gamekeeper shot the varmint and, after backfilling, carried the carcass away. Bruiser's next opponent would be more of a problem.

Early that season, hounds crossed the fields to draw a dense spinney but, even before they reached there, two foxes were away, rising from the cover in a corner of the meadow. They rushed through a gap in the hedge as the hounds, finding the scent, began their cry. The foxes were running almost alongside each other and ran towards the quiet road. A small vixen and a big, strong, athletic red fox. A fox with only one ear. Tom had recognised Cadno immediately and could hardly contain his excitement.

They were out of sight now, and the scent did not seem too good for the hounds had slowed, but then Cadno and the vixen were spotted, not thirty yards apart, running slowly, struggling in places, up the almost vertically sloping bank. They had not intended to tackle that difficult climb but had been turned from their chosen path by a farmer, who was leaning on the gate which they were hoping to pass through. They entered a patch of thick gorse when they cleared the cliff-like slope and as hounds came to the area, they stopped, casting about before marking furiously at an extensive earth.

Tom soon arrived, with Bruiser on a lead and, tying him to a tree began to block every hole he could find. He guessed that the vixen would have gone to ground but that Cadno would surely, still be running, making sure of his escape. The hounds were taken from the earth and stood, or sat, quietly above the gorse bank as Bruiser forced his way into the tight tunnels.

In a matter of moments, he had located his opponent and a tremendous struggle began. Tom, four feet above Bruiser, heard the sounds of conflict and started to dig. Intermingled with the barks of the terrier, were his cries of frustration and pain. He had met his toughest opponent yet, in his short life. Pressed flat to the floor of the tunnel, Bruiser's jaw rested on the earth as he attempted to force his way up a slight incline, to get close to the fox, hidden behind a sharp bend.

The terrier was constricted and could hardly raise his head to get leverage, and each time he forced forward, he was punished for his enterprise by the fox which, by chance, had taken up a near-invincible position. Again and again, the terrier attempted to edge right up to his opponent, but every time he did so, the fox peppered his muzzle until his face was bloodied and sore. The sounds of the digging were nearing the two animals and Bruiser, in his determination, turned onto his back and forced his way, once more, towards the fox. Now, he faced upwards, looking towards his opponent though he could see nothing in the pitch darkness of the sett. But he could strike back. As the terrier's head came within reach, the fox tried once more for a punishing grip, but this time, instead of striking at the unprotected, upper muzzle, there were jaws that could retaliate and Bruiser gained his first grip on his opponent.

Ten minutes later, Tom opened the hole and lifted the terrier and the lifeless form of the vixen, from the earth. They were both covered in clay, wet and bedraggled, and as Tom threw the carcass to the top of the bank, to reward the waiting hounds, a second fox sprang from the workings and fled away, under the gorse, like a red flash. One ear was missing, and Tom cursed himself. He should have known that both foxes were somewhere in the tunnels. Bruiser had been keen to re-enter, trying to free himself from Tom's grip and anyway, if one fox had continued to run, at least half of the pack would have followed. They would not *all* have marked the earth.

Cadno appeared to lead a charmed life. He was almost as fortunate as Tom had been, to serve, unharmed through the years of warfare. His time had not yet come and though the hounds, leaving the dead vixen, had pursued with enthusiasm, he was more than a match for them in his familiar countryside and he used his knowledge to his best advantage. The chase lasted for an hour and ended when Cadno entered a field of cattle. The animals followed him to the far side, as if drawn by an irresistible force and when the hounds came to the field, all trace of the musky scent had been obliterated.

Tom had been left alone at the gorse patch when the hunt continued and he could only reflect and marvel that such a relatively small vixen, weighing about thirteen pounds, had been able to wreak such havoc upon his best terrier.

Though Bruiser's weight only just exceeded hers, he had been able to prove his superiority against foxes of twenty pounds and more, and his meetings with the badger meant that he usually faced an animal of at least twenty-five pounds. The muscle tone and bone structure of the terrier made him much stronger than the average fox though he could never hope to match the tank-like badger, if it came to a trial of strength. When faced with the badger, a terrier needed his wits about him and sheer strength was never enough. There were foxes, and there were foxes, and when their attitude was one of aggression, then it proved to Tom that even a small vixen could present a terrier with a difficult task, holed up in a favourable place. What price then, when a specimen like Cadno, fearless to the point of foolhardiness at times, lay in wait for an animal that did not have one hundred per cent commitment?

Tom had the utmost respect for their courage and ability and admired them as a species for their tenacious fight for survival when everything, and, it seemed, everybody, was dedicated to their destruction. Though the battle had not lasted very long, Bruiser, not yet completely fit, was exhausted and followed at Tom's heels, forcing his weary frame, willing himself to keep up with his master.

Tom was halfway across the field when he noticed Bruiser was not with him. He waited a while and called and whistled but the dog did not appear. His owner returned to the gorse and, searching, found a small earth, with just one entrance. He could hear the terrier as he bayed, just a short way in. Kneeling, he tried to reach the terrier, grasping at the tail, but he was just out of reach and so Tom had no option but to dig along the shallow tube until he came to the dog.

Bruiser lay stretched along the passage, baying as if his very life depended on it and, as he did, his tail wagged from side to side, like a metronome. Tom had a good idea of the quarry and, as he withdrew the dog, he placed the blade of the shovel to block the hole until he had a collar and lead fastened to Bruiser.

Soon, the striped head and bright black eyes of a badger came into view and, removing the spade, Tom stood aside, holding Bruiser firmly, allowing the badger to lumber away, back into the gorse patch, to resume his disturbed rest period elsewhere. It looked like a young boar, probably newly independent from his birth sett and intent upon establishing his own place and, in time, his own family.

Bruiser had to be half-dragged, struggling all the way, for the next fifty yards, until he gave up his efforts to release himself to resume the hunt for his foe. Then, remembering his fatigue, he allowed himself to be led, listlessly along. In the years ahead, he would develop into a superb terrier for digging to brock but before that, he had many hard lessons to be learned and lived a digging life that would have totally discouraged and spoiled a less determined, lesser spirited animal. His breeding would tell. His blood lines were of the best. Bred right, he would stay right.

He worked his way through a sort of mental crash barrier, and settled to the job until, at his best, he would work, sustaining hardly any injuries, bottling up badgers and keeping them occupied until they could be bagged and moved or, as a last resort, humanely destroyed, having suffered no harm in the interim process. Tom and Bruiser had no way of foreseeing the future, when savages and brutes would prostitute the simple, even sympathetic method until it came to be looked upon as a vile ritual practiced by inhuman sadists.

Tom walked on in silence, deep in thought. What mysterious force made such terriers give of their best until they were physically shattered and then, hardly able to walk, give more, return to work, start another task? It was the almost omnipotent force of determination which certain animals called to their assistance when adversity struck its hardest blows. The strange force which raised the almost beaten prize fighter from the canvas to claim a victory which he would not be denied. The same force which drove men to fight back from ruin and despair and forge a new life. The force which could not be conquered, and would never be contained.

When he arrived home, he cleaned the dog, washing his face, his mouth, his eyes, clearing debris from his coat and applying soothing ointment to his cuts. Then he allowed Bruiser's daughter to come into the house and the dog made no protest when she lay beside him, and soon she was busy with her tongue, cleansing and soothing the tired warrior, like a mother hen. Both terriers ate a good supper and settled down before the fire, close to their master's feet. They were content and could not ask for more. The love of Bruiser for his owner was returned in full measure and Tom forever gloried in the ability of the terrier. Not for the manner, or the number of foxes he accounted for, but for everything, every nuance, that went to make up the whole, the complete, working terrier.

Tom was a compassionate man and would resent anyone who described him as cruel. He did a job which had to be done and the man and the terrier did it to the best of their ability, with as little suffering as possible.

One day, Tom expected to meet his maker, to stand, humbly, before an almighty presence. He did not want to do so in shame. He did not want to have to apologise for the way he had chosen to live his hard, uncompromising life.

Chapter 14

Farewell Good Bitch

As the holly trees came into full splendour, hung with scarlet berries, ready for the approach of Christmas, Ruby, in her old age, began to struggle to keep up with the pack. All her life she had been at the front, even from her first season. She had caught foxes on the run, she had dug them from small earths, she had followed them deep into the far reaches of badger setts too vast to dig, she had made it her sole purpose to seek out the fox and end his life, whenever she could. Now, after just a short run, other hounds passed her. Left her far behind.

The huntsman was the first to notice her decline and saw the old head drop as she struggled to keep up. She would still be the first to find, still be the last to leave an earth when hounds marked, but in between, her limbs grew stiff.

Her time had passed.

Her mother had been the star of the pack and her mother's mother, before. Now, in the kennel, the continuation of the tried and tested old blood was entrusted to Ruby's son and two daughters. Next year, they would enter, to run with the pack, but they would never run beside their mother.

Cadno was becoming careless, a fault no fox could hope to get away with for long. Perhaps it was because he was rarely a lone fox any longer. He spent an increasing amount of time in the company of his own kind and only recently, he had been asleep in a badger sett and had not stirred until a terrier was almost upon him. His vixen had not joined him in the earth, preferring to shelter in some heavy cover and she had moved quickly to safety when the two men with terriers came over the fields. The shrill yap of the terrier brought him quickly to his senses and he charged, recklessly and violently, for it had become almost a reflex action when danger threatened. Slowly he forced the terrier from the earth. The two men were surprised.

"Must be a badger" said the younger of the two, "let another dog in, dad," and his father had loosed a strong-looking white dog to join the black and tan bitch. There was just room enough for both to work side by side and, bolstered by each other's presence, their excited barking almost deafened Cadno in the enclosed space. Again he charged, suddenly, furiously, and, hampered by their own cramped bodies, the terriers could not avoid his charge. He stuck at the dog and gashed the white face, forcing him to recoil and then he bit violently at the bitch and both terriers were soon in retreat. A third dog was let in but the result was just the same. The men could scent the fox and had seen his muzzle in the darkness of the tunnel as he followed the curs to the entrance. They were determined to kill him. But they had no terriers capable of working to this hell-fox that knew no fear and trounced them. To be fair, they were rabbiters, not earth dogs, used against the fox only rarely and though they could be relied on to mark a bury where the rabbit was in residence, or kill rats by the score, they had not the heart for the danger and hardship of the earth-terrier's occupation when the job was difficult and required sustained courage.

The younger man ran down the valley and returned half an hour later, with four gin traps. Setting them, he used a stick to push one into each entrance, using a long cord to fasten it to a bush or a tree, to restrain the captive animal when it was caught. It might take some time, but they had him now. There was no escape for Cadno, and the men went on their way.

As evening fell, the fox investigated each entrance but he would not attempt to go past the traps. He had an aversion to steel and the scent of man was strong on them. He would wait, though, already, hunger gnawed at him and prodded him to take a risk.

Before an hour had passed, he was free.

A fat young boar badger, inquisitive and seeking some digging work for his strong paws, came blundering into the sett and he did not hesitate, in spite of the lingering terrier scent. In he went trundling over a trap and then racing away in terror, snapping the cord to which it was attached, like a thread of cotton as the steel jaws closed about the fine hairs of his under belly. Before he had gone fifty yards, the trap, lacking a proper grip, fell away, holding just a clump of body hair and brock, free from its presence, slowed his hectic retreat and comforted himself by searching for his supper.

Within half an hour, Cadno had left the sett, unharmed, thanks to the unintentional assistance of the young boar. Was it arrogance and the pride of a fox in his prime that caused him to disregard the lesson? Still he was careless, and soon the Garth Valley hounds marked him to ground in a sett above a rocky outcrop. Where was the lifeblood of his ancestors which flowed in his veins and in every living fibre? Had his senses temporarily deserted him?

The weather was wet. Wet and vicious, with mean, gale-force winds and rain that never stopped and it seemed to the fox that he spent his entire life below the ground. He should have heard the hounds, should have been aware of their approach, but the vixen was the first to react. She had heard the huntsman's voice as he encouraged the pack, calling to them, and she immediately began to move through the tunnels, in a panic. Soon the hounds were marking strongly and, taking a chance, she bolted from the top entrance, unseen for the first twenty yards.

The huntsman viewed her and screamed to the hounds and, lifting their heads from the earth, they were off, in full pursuit. All, except old Ruby.

She had forced her way into the earth and showed no intention of coming out. Tom had arrived by now and, alone, he stood watching the rear end of the bitch as she struggled in the passages, which, for a hound, were exceptionally tight. Was she trying to force her way in or attempting to back out? It was hard to tell. He knew what Bruiser wanted to do. The terrier strained at his leash, eager to be free, but was he excited by the actions of the hound or was he simply stirred by the strong scent of the vixen which had gone away? Tom let him loose and he flew into the earth, passing Ruby who wriggled out to let him pass. As Bruiser went in, Cadno came out, not two yards away, from another entrance, and Ruby lunged at him. Had she been younger, the fox would have died then, but her reactions had slowed and he twisted aside, jumping high, and then Bruiser shot out from the same hole.

Cadno leapt onto the rocks and fled, skating over the rough, rugged surface as the hound and the terrier floundered, left standing for speed by the cat-like agility of the fox. Bruiser followed for half a mile and then returned to Tom.

Ruby had gone forever.

In her blind, determined quest for her quarry, she followed with all the speed her old limbs could muster, as if rejuvenated, for one last run. She followed to the old lead mine and she followed to the cliff face and there, high above, she saw Cadno, climbing, running, jumping and twisting along the narrow paths and ledges. Soon, she too was near the top and then, as she tired, she slipped on the loose shale of a narrow shelf. She scrabbled desperately to maintain her balance, clawing to regain her foothold. She strained every sinew and her nails scraped at the wet rock and then, slowly at first, she slid from the track, plunging over the edge, down, down, headlong, to land with a sickening, dull thud which broke her old bones and crushed the lifeblood from her kind old head, and sent her hound-soul to eternity.

The stout-hearted, docile hound would hunt her homeland no more and the day, which had began with clouds in the sky, ended with clouds in the hearts and minds of her huntsman, and all who had watched her and admired her over her many seasons.

Cadno, careless Cadno, had escaped once again, but his most recent vixen partner had fallen to the relentless fury of the pack as they followed the strong scent and pulled her down in full flight. Dana had caught her, and Delyth, Major Bach, Raleigh and Radnor, Sandy and Julie were quickly on the scene.

Tom helped to bury the old hound, close to where she had fallen, just at the edge of the quarry floor, and it would be many

Cadno.

seasons before they passed the scene without thinking of her, and remembering.

Tom Flanders had been taught two more lessons, which he should have already learned. Silence and caution. The fox was always one step ahead. Human voices had made the vixen bolt, giving her early warning. Then, when Bruiser and Ruby had been so keen, he should have quickly blocked the holes, or netted them, before releasing the terrier to search the sett. It was easy to be wise when it was too late, but difficult to remain calm and act, always correctly, in the tense, stirring atmosphere when life, or death, for the fox, depended on the right decision.

Cadno had survived, in spite of his carelessness. Tom had also been careless and would need to be wide awake, alive, alert if he hoped to account for this fox with the savaged ear, which was beginning to be more than a challenge. Cadno had become a quest, a crusade, for Tom and his terrier. He must fall to no other.

* * * * *

And Cadno moved again and lived at risk, under an outbuilding in an old widow's back garden, and he fed on scraps which she left for the birds and he rummaged through her waste bin and she became aware of his presence and begun to leave out bowls of milk and other tasty morsels.

At first, he had thought the place to be uninhabited, there were few signs of occupation. There was a warm, dry cavity beneath the floor of the byre and the fox used it, just for the moment, a convenient resting place, as he would make use of any cover which suited him. He lay there most of the day and was not disturbed. There was no sound, no movement, just an overgrown garden with a dilapidated, decaying bird table at one end, and some china dishes scattered about, half empty and encrusted with mould and rotting food particles. There were plenty of mice, and he caught them with an almost nonchalant ease, eating his fill and burying surplus kills in various locations. He had no reason to move on, and three days later, the first bowl of milk appeared. He drank it quickly, lapping at it greedily, unaware of the eyes which watched him, with pleasure, from the kitchen window.

Miss Lacy, as she was known, had worked as ladies' maid at the mansion, until her failing health had forced her to give up, but she lived on, rent free, in her cottage, her well-being still being taken care of by the family she had served so well. She kept her house clean and tidy but the garden had become too great a burden and she spent much of her time watching the birds she attracted to the overgrown patch, fast becoming a wilderness.

Blue tits, great tits, robins, thrush and blackbirds, chaffinch, wagtail, nuthatch and woodpecker and scores more. She knew many by their individual mannerisms and had even managed to coax the cheeky blue tits to feed from her hand when the winter had been severe and birds had struggled to avoid starvation. Now she had a fox to study. And what had happened to his ear? He had been in the wars. She hoped he would stay and did her best to make him welcome but when an underkeeper brought her a parcel from the mansion, he sensed fox presence immediately and soon searched for the hideout and read the tell-tale signs and scents of droppings and half buried small animals. He told her of her guest and she feigned innocence, pretending surprise when he told her that he would be back to set snares, bringing Tom with his terriers. She wanted him to live.

When next she saw the fox, she frightened him badly, shouting and screaming, and then she disturbed the privacy of the cover around his small earth, pushing bundles of paper into the main entrance, and setting them to smoulder, so that Cadno moved on once more, and when Tom called with his terriers, there was no longer any sign of the visitor.

Chapter 15

The Circle of Life

They were well into winter.

Soon it would be Christmas, but to Cadno, all it meant was that days grew shorter until they reached their limit and then began, almost imperceptibly, to lengthen once more. And vixens became more interesting.

He had soon found company after leaving the earth in the byre. He was rarely alone and enjoyed meeting his fellow foxes and, at this special time, in the depths of winter, his fellow foxes welcomed him. At least the vixens did. Some of the dog foxes were surly and resented him, but he was big and strong and none dared to challenge him.

He surrounded himself with his harem and once had the attentions of three fawning vixens but, when their combined presence overwhelmed him, he would go off to hunt alone, glorying once more in the independence and solitude he had enjoyed in his youth.

The Boxing Day meet took place at the Angel Inn and followers came from far and near. Tom had transport now. He had bought a curious three-wheeled contraption, half-way between a van and a motor cycle. It had one wheel at the front and was steered with handle bars inside the snub-nosed cab. It could hardly be described as a glamourous carriage and yet it made a huge difference to the man and his terriers. He could follow hounds much more closely, anticipating their direction and hurrying along the quiet roads and lanes to stay in touch. It seemed as though every supporter, every member, had turned out that day and the little inn was crowded. Though the hunt was not a smart, fashionable, well-known one, there were over two hundred subscribing members and they valued the fox control work which the huntsman carried out on their behalf.

There was plenty to eat, plenty to drink, songs were sung, and the master gave a little speech. He thanked the people for coming, thanked them for their support throughout the year, praised the huntsman and his hounds and rounded it off with a toast to the fox. Never was a creature so loved and so hated, so admired and so despised, never was an animal so pursued, so persecuted and yet, in the final resort, so protected. None wished his extinction. No fox. No hunting. The countryside, and those who lived and worked it, knew it to unthinkable.

But his numbers had to be kept to a reasonable level.

The huntsman, followed by his hounds, rode out of the village and made a heart-warming sight. Many of the observers came only for this moment and never followed any further, but to all, whatever the measure of their involvement, the hunt was a part of country living, essential, everlasting.

The day was dark, foreboding, and heavy hail showers drove into the huntsman's face but, as he made his first draw, the sky cleared, bright and blue though the clouds, like cotton wool, were scudding across the sky. He followed the pack over the wet meadow and the sinking bog and he drew through bracken and gorse, encouraging the hounds with his voice, rarely sounding the horn. A pale sun ventured from behind a heavy, black cloud, peering cautiously as if uncertain of its authority to make an appearance, and smiling shyly as the hounds clamoured, taking turns to press through a gap in the hedge.

Down into the little valley and the clouds crouched threateningly, before a rising wind. There was no shelter to be found and gusts forced their way into heavy coats and thick shirts, chilling the huntsman as he battled on across the open field, head held low, turned against the gathering storm. The wind sang a mournful song and sent the rain flying before it, twisting and turning across the fields. Animals shrank behind trees and hedges and dripping sheep stood flat under the sheltering stone walls and suddenly, Dana and Teifi gave voice, joined immediately by the rest of the pack, soprano Dana, bass Radnor, the warbling treble tones of Sandy and Julie and the triumphant tenor voice, loud and clear, of Ranger. The concert had begun, and the glorious choir sang and Cadno and his vixens, lying warm and dry, left their refuge and scattered before the wind, like driven autumn leaves. The weather was ignored, and the hunt was on.

Four foxes. They had risen together and divided immediately, taking two different directions, Cadno and his special vixen headed for the river and, though it was fast-running, made angry by the extraordinary rainfall of the past weeks, they plunged in without hesitation, being swept downstream for a hundred yards before gaining the other side. They were safe. The huntsman, quick to see the danger, had prevented the pack from splitting, and they had gone away fast, in pursuit of the two remaining vixens.

Before much distance had been covered, these two went their separate ways and though three hounds fell away, after the weaker, the bulk of the pack did not hesitate or deviate from the line, and remained on the scent of the bigger, stronger female.

Two miles she ran and then she turned and came back in a circle, and as she did so was headed by some followers and turned her mask to the dark forest of Maerdy, with its many earths.

When Tom arrived, bumping up the rough track in his motor, the hounds had blocked all the entrances and dug fresh trenches at every likely tube. Roots had been ripped asunder and the site took his mind, fleetingly, to a time of deeper trenches, thicker mud, and more certain death. For the merest instant, he turned back the years and scented, not the fox, or the hounds, but the rotting, decaying stench of Flanders. He saw troops giving stupid "thumbs-up" signs before they marched in their thousands to certain extermination and then, in a flash, he was in the prize ring and the thumb, enclosed in a glove, was gouging at his eye and the liniment and arc lights and solitude were real before him, and then he came back to reality, tying Bruiser to a tree, looking for the best place to start the search for the fox. He was shaken, but did not show it. He looked about, but no one had appeared to notice him, or give him a curious glance. His mental trip to another time, his secrets, were still his own.

It took almost half and hour before they could find an opening to enter the terrier, but at last, they cleared a way, and Bruiser pushed in. Fifteen minutes late, another vixen life had been claimed and the hunters now realising that they were soaked to the skin, lost no time in returning to the inn to drive the chill from their bones.

Tom joined them, indulging himself for once, but when he went to his bed that night, the liquor failed to give him oblivion, or rest. The year was coming to an end. It had been a good year, but questions still remained to be answered in his subconscious mind. Questions which had remained unanswered for many years and, perhaps, would never be resolved.

* * * * *

Cadno and his special vixen were rarely separated.

They hunted together and rested together and as she came into the mating condition, he guarded her jealously and warned away all potential competition for her favours. They braved the wild storms of January and settled gradually into their territory until they knew every rock and every stream and every pathway and hedge. They were free from the cries of the hounds and the terrible hunting times faded to a distant memory as they enjoyed each other's company. Cadno was her lord and master, her monarch of the wild woods, and she supplicated herself to his being, doing his bidding and living beneath his shadow. For his part, he watched over her and taught her to be wary where gaps led easily through hedges, where gifted meals lay deliciously tempting and where incautious steps could bring savage pain. His careless time was past and in his maturity came the wisdom of the ages and the intuitive cunning of his tribe.

February brought its blizzards and, as his fourth birthday approached he knew again the deprivation of hunger. In the snows of the early month, badger sows gave life to small litters and warmed them deep below the frozen, white blanketed surface, in caverns where their boars would not be welcomed until their cubs were older. His own vixen wife was with cub, but her time was not yet, and her birthing would not occur until late March when hedgerows prepared to dress themselves in their spring greenery as the small birds inclined their instincts to their pairing and nest making times, fast approaching, and the daffodils and primrose usurped the brief reign of the snowdrops.

First she must survive the deathly cold hands of snow and frost and Cadno must help her, to ensure a healthy, strong, litter, to continue his line.

* * * * *

He had lived through a cold time with another vixen.

He had known the joy of cubs, and the despair of loss.

All life was a circle. There was nothing new. When the land turned white and the cold carpet lay in place, foxes had to be extra cautious. Everywhere they went, their footprints followed, marked sharply in the snow, and the comings and goings of just one pair, could inspire a farmer with fear of an invasion of dozens. Eight feet. To and fro, backwards and forwards, and when stockmen saw the signs near henhouses, they set their gins, and carried their guns and kennelled their dogs nearby, on running lines.

Cadno was hungry, but his vixen fed for seven, for she carried six cubs in her belly and craved nourishment. Beneath the snow, the ground was hard, unyielding, and hunting for food was a daunting task which brought foxes ever nearer to man and his habitations. Cadno skirted the pheasant coverts, placing himself in great danger, even though he took extreme care. Gamekeepers were alert and on duty at all hours and their silent sentinels, the trap, the snare, were ever primed to end the life of the careless predator. On the edge of a small field, underneath a large, twisted oak, the fox saw the briefest movement and a flash of colour, though he was unable to discern red from green or brown. Instantly, he became motionless. He had stopped in mid-stride, and watched, intent, gazing at the place, now still, where something had stirred. For long moments he maintained his pose and then he saw again, the merest movement. A plump cock pheasant sheltered in the shadow of the tree's huge girth.

Cadno could not cross the field, there was no cover to make use of. He would be easily seen, a russet form moving over a white backcloth. Carefully, but as quickly as stealth allowed, he hugged the hedges until, soon, he was near the oak. The pheasant scratched at the ground, moving the rotting acorns and leaves, probing with his beak, and as he was thus occupied, Cadno edged nearer. Cautiously, cleverly, he came within striking distance and then the cock pheasant saw his murderer. In panic, he ran, in fright, he tried to fly, but as he gained height and as his strident cry clanged out, Cadno became a blur, leaping through the air and bringing the handsome bird crashing, crunching to the ground. He crushed the chest and bit at the throat and the pheasant died in a mess of feathers.

A shot rang out and a loud voice shouted but the keeper, though he had been concealed, was much too far away and could do nothing as Cadno, arrogant, with the bird in his mouth, ran off. He was too hungry to be frightened into discarding his prize and soon he was gone from sight. He did not stop until he was joined by his vixen, more than half a mile away, and when they had finished, all that remained was a few feathers in the blood-stained, paw-marked snow.

They lived in an earth under the stone floor of an abandoned chapel. Once the building had reverberated to the hymns of praise and the hwyl of the minister. Now, the roof had collapsed and the windows and doors had rotted and roots and ivy had forced their way between the stones of the walls. Rain, frost and ice had weakened the structure and some of the dressed stones had even been taken to shore up walls, and to repair farm buildings. No one ever came near the place and rabbits had excavated an extensive burrow. It was dry, secure, warm. The stone floor served as a strong roof over the tunnels below. They were safe. As safe as a fox could be.

The weather would not relent and the cold time continued. Even the lazy badgers, cushioned with their layers of store fat, began to grumble, and the lesser creatures began to die. Hares loped around the countryside like bony, scrawny bags of fur and buzzards called plaintively from grey skies as their keen eyes searched the barren, blinding-white lands below. Birds died and made pitiful, dry eating for foxes, and ponds and streams froze over, causing the vulnerable herons, already gaunt, to waste away. The scavengers, the carrion eaters, that kept the countryside clean and fresh, knew want and hardship and the least morsel became a valued prize, sustaining life, maintaining hope.

The snare had been robbed again. Five days ago, a badger sow, rapidly losing her covering of fat flesh, had fed well on the captive rabbit, leaving little trace of her meal, which she devoured where she found it. It had been pillaged again, but this time the thief was Cadno, who had accepted the gift with gratitude, tearing it from the snare and carrying it back to share with his vixen at the chapel. Though she was often hungry and did not feed as well as she would have wished, her body had started to fill out and Cadno, masterful though he was, became very proud and grew even more conscious of his responsibilities. Last year's cubs had been lost. He would ensure, to the best of his abilities, the survival of the new litter. He would never again live a lonely life. Solitude, for him, was over.

Chapter 16

The Hand of Fate

As the thaw set in, as the dead hand of deep winter eased its grip, Cadno carried another prize to the vixen. The bright mallard drake had died quickly at the edge of the marsh, and gradually, conditions, for the wild things, became less arduous.

Soon the bare earth would recover, discarding its suffocating blanket. It had benefited from its rest and would soon burst into life, and new born wildlings would begin their precarious progress through life.

The vixen's time was near.

Already some of her kind had cubbed and at one earth, a young litter fed on meat though Cadno's cubs had not been born. His vixen became restless and sought out a suitable nursery. With Cadno close at hand, she examined earths for suitability and scraped out many before rejecting them, and in her turbulent, agitated condition, she killed her first lamb.

She did not eat it.

It was simply a senseless reaction, and she left the carcass where it had fallen, on the far, open hill. It was not discovered until two days had elapsed and by then the carrion eaters had mutilated it, and she had killed again, on another farm. The crime came to the farmer's attention the next day but, even if he had searched, she would not have been found, for her travels at this time were unpredictable and she herself had no idea of her destinations. At last, she had made her choice and entered the earth to prepare for the time to give life. Cadno would not see her again, until the whelps had been born.

The second lamb had been killed near Tom's cottage and he had tried every known earth within easy reach, but the terriers did not mark at any. Some of the refuges were scratched out and this had been done as the vixen searched for her suitable birth chamber. They still carried her lingering scent and Tom let the terriers explore carefully, allowing them time to be certain that no fox was in residence. In one small copse, a jay flew raucously away and Cadno, resting at the far end, was grateful for the warning of man's presence and skulked over the hill without being seen.

Soon the bare earth would recover.

And when Tom returned to his cottage, a letter had been pushed under his door. The neat handwriting, and the postmark, were immediately recognisable and he carried it into the kitchen, opening it carefully, slitting it with a knife, then, taking it to the fire, he settled himself in his armchair and removed it from the envelope.

He had known it was from Jane before he picked it off the doormat. He had need of a woman in his life. Man is a social creature and, like all living things, flourishes in the company of his own kind. Tom had thought his life to be complete in every way, but had come to realise it was not so. He planted and tended his vegetables, feeding cheaply on the results of his labour. He threw meal to his chickens and gathered their eggs, and watched a red hen as she hatched a clutch of eggs in her secret place in the hedge. He was industrious and filled his winter wood store with logs, allowing them to dry out during the summer months so that they would burn over the coal more brightly through the deep winter. But, in many ways, he was less fortunate than the creatures of the wild land who knew the intimate company of their own kind, and lived as nature had ordained.

He had fought against, and triumphed over, a great deal of adversity in his life, but he had always striven to maintain his basic, optimistic outlook, with varying degrees of success. He was no student of psychology and yet he had realised, long ago, that this quality of life, reflecting his thoughts, suffered when he became morose and introvert. "Anyone can sing when the sun shines", he would say, but what really counted was the way in which you could cope with life when things were not going well, and when everything seemed to be working against him, he would strive, all the more, to keep his mind contented. It would be so much easier with Jane at his side. He had been hasty when he had written to her after her second bereavement. She had needed time to weep, time to adjust, time to respectfully lay aside another chapter of her life.

The letter was carefully composed.

Tom imagined her, seated at her kitchen table, writing, correcting, until she was satisfied. Every word had to be exact, precise. She would have spent some time over its content and then, she would have copied it out, careful to make no errors, in her neat, compact style.

She apologised for her hasty, abrupt reply to his earlier offer. She had been upset, unsettled. Did he understand? Did he intend to visit the valley soon? She had never had a holiday, needed a break from her mind-numbing routine. Was he enjoying his life in the country? She wanted to see him.

It was more, far more, than he had dared to hope for, but neither of them were young and they had wasted enough time. How typical of her that she should take a bold initiative when her course of action came clearly to her mind. It was a reflection of her strength of character, of her determination, like Tom, to overcome misfortune and wrest from life that which she unwaveringly saw as her destiny. Tom had always shaped his own life, setting himself targets, and, apart from the period when he had been forced from the ring, he had lived as he had chosen to live and if conditions did not suit, he had only himself, and his thoughts, to blame. He created his own environment and he realised, yet again, that his dominant, subconscious thoughts were about to be brought into effect. It was, in many ways, uncanny, and yet, the results of his private science could not be denied.

His reply would tell her that he *would* revisit the valley as soon as the danger to the lambing fields was over. He told her of the beauty of his surroundings and of the kindly, honest manner of his people. He quoted from the bible, reverting, for inspiration, as always, to his childhood in the chapel. "And the greatest of these is charity," and he copied from his well-worn dictionary, defining charity as a kindly attitude towards ones fellow men, an overwhelming love of mankind and, without saying so, he hoped that she realised that he did, indeed, offer love. A mature love, an understanding love, a love that would survive all minor upheavals and petty frustrations. An abiding, serious love that could complete his life and add colour to his, and her, future years.

* * * * *

To a casual observer, the steep, sloping hillside was a tangled wilderness of brambles, bracken and dead or decaying branches. Passages and tunnels entered at all sides and beneath the undergrowth, a veritable maze developed, like a network of highways, for the use of small animals, up to the size of the fox, or the badger. Terriers might brave the thorny openings but larger dogs, hounds, or sheepdogs, or lurchers, had little hope of penetrating its interior. In the middle of it all, in the deep inner underworld, away from the weak whiteness of the moon and the shimmering stars, the vixen lay exhausted and worn, racked by the pain of a difficult birth-time.

She had not complained.

She had made no sound of protest, not even the merest whimper, for foxes are able to endure their tribulations in silence and are known to die quietly, even in a maelstrom. Six cubs, but the first, the cause of her trials, had been born devoid of life and had so taxed her strength that the remainder, though alive, had also been difficult. Another would soon perish and already she had rejected its cooling form, pushing it away from her side, knowing it was beyond her assistance. Of the remainder, two were weak little mewlings, but one dog and one vixen were strong and sturdy and would certainly thrive.

These two suckled vigorously and pushed aside their weaker kin, resting on the warmth of the vixen's teats, anchored to her life-giving milk by the strong suction of their curved tongues and their clamping, firm little jaws. The vixen drifted into a shallow sleep, waking regularly and cleaning, polishing her whelps with her kindly tongue. For two days she cossetted them and the tiny specimens slowly improved, for her milk was plentiful and they gained weight and grew until they were almost a match for their more fortunate litter mates who had made a better start.

Cadno visited the bury but did not enter, though he listened intently at the entrance, cocking his head to one side. On the third night, his patience, his curiosity was rewarded and his mate dragged herself, stiffly, to meet him, greedily consuming the small rabbit he had provided for her. He licked at her and began to groom her dishevelled coat but she did not stay long and, after relieving herself, she hurried back to her cubs, lying alone on the bare earth in the confines of the birth chamber.

For the next week, the dog fox provided for his mate and then, for the first time since the birth, they hunted together as the vixen left her cubs alone. Soon the youngsters opened their tight eyelids and peered weakly at their confined world through blue eyes. The dusky faces and poker-like tails began to register their emotions, showing pleasure and pain, joy and apprehension and, as the small teeth created soreness at the vixen's teats, she began to regurgitate meals for them, introducing them to solid food.

The mother had deteriorated badly and her condition had suffered as she allowed the litter to suckle her strength away. Perhaps the cold time, with its hardship, had not allowed her to prepare as well as she would have liked but soon her milk grew less and the cub's growing appetites demanded more than she could provide. Her pelt developed raw, bare patches and she scratched constantly at her belly which had become very tender, due to the attentions of the needle sharp teeth of her growing family.

She needed to build herself back to health and strength, for never was there a more bedraggled looking mother. Every night she left her litter and searched for sustenance for herself and the little ones. Every night they hunted together, the weakened vixen and the proud Cadno, but food was not easy to find. The harsh winter had taken a high toll of wild creatures and nature would need time to replace its lost children.

The two foxes ran at hares, in desperation, and scavenged far and wide but they faced competition from others of their kind for the search for food knew no boundaries when hunger came upon them. More than one fox perished at the hands of the keepers as the pheasants came under threat and raids on well-protected henhouses were unproductive, as well as dangerous.

It was left to the lambing fields to provide the quickest, easiest meals but here again, the ultimate price was often paid for a full belly. Cadno hunted every waking hour. He was driven by the obsession of raising a litter of cubs and keeping them safe from the attentions of his enemies. Already he played contentedly with his offspring and, in the eyes of his partner, placed none above the other but, though he did not show it, he looked with special favour on his strong young son and anticipated the time when he would help his vixen to rear them and pass on his wisdom and wood-wiseness.

He spared no effort in his quest for food but there was never enough to be found. Within less than a square mile, three other vixens raised their families and there were just too many mouths to feed adequately.

Hunger gripped at the cubs and curled its thin, grasping fingers about them. Their craving for nourishment made them ever more daring and demanding in their cries and Cadno decided it was time for him to take a desperate chance. As darkness settled over the land, as the clouds obscured the moon, he set out to bring food in plenty to his vixen and his children. He would visit the lambing fields.

He moved silently and swiftly through the shadowed land, instinctively using all the available cover and as he crossed the narrow, shallow, rapidly flowing stream, the scents of the ewes and their recently born lambs came heavily to his excited, twitching nostrils. It was time for extreme caution and he took the utmost care not to disturb the ewes more than he could help.

Soon, he came upon two new-born lambs and their wearied mother. The twins were still sticky from their birthtime and were hardly steady on their feet and Cadno singled out the larger of the two for his special attention. This lamb walked on stronger legs and would be easier to part from its mother. He moved towards it but the ewe manoeuvred herself between them, stamping at the ground angrily. Cadno showed no concern, and passed easily by but then, he charged at the smaller lamb. The mother moved to guard the new threat and the fox deftly placed himself between the ewe and the bigger lamb. Expertly he drove the frightened creature further from the frantic ewe, who tried vainly to protect him but Cadno would simply turn his attention to the smaller animal and again, in her helplessness, the ewe would move to guard it. A large distance soon separated the two lambs, and the fox, deadly in his savagery, immediately drove the doomed lamb before him. In an instant, he was at its throat and ended the brief life of the snow-white lamb without further ceremony. He dragged the lifeless body to the gate and, tearing at the stomach, ate part of the soft entrails before carrying it back on the long journey to his cubs.

He paid not the slightest attention to the ewe, bleating plaintively, and gave no thought to the consequences of his barbarous raid. That night, the cubs and their mother would feast, and all would be well with his growing family.

Carrying the lamb, pausing only occasionally to rest and shift his grip, he came to the earth and as he did, even as he pushed into the undergrowth, the cubs, throwing all caution aside, darted out of the darkness to meet him. They wrestled the lamb from his jaws, even before he could release it and fought in the most determined manner over their share of the tasty prize. The noise of their squabbling carried far in the stillness of the night and stealthy creatures of the darkness hastened about their business in alarm. The cubs would have to be taught better behaviour. Soon, they had all claimed their portions and scattered to eat it, each seeking a secluded spot where they could eat and keep a watch on their kin at the same time.

Cadno watched them, his face expressionless, his manner as ever, alert and wary. He saw no sign of the vixen and so, with a last glance at his children he faded, unnoticed into the night. It was time to find his own supper.

Before the dawn, he had returned to the family home, carrying a fat rabbit. The spirit of the woodland had, at last, relented, travelling with him during his hours of hunting and showering him with its bounty. He had feasted on young mice and a half-grown rabbit before cornering his last victim in a stop end of a stony warren.

Had his fortune improved just one night earlier, he may never have had to take the lamb, but by such chance does fate select its victims, though the dog fox was unaware of the fact. He dropped the meal at the end of the tangle and moved to the hillside where he sat for some time on his haunches, cleaning his paws and face. He saw the vixen as she came from the bracken to claim the rabbit and the manner in which she tore hungrily at it, eating part of it before dragging the remainder in to the cubs, told him plainly that her hunting had been less successful than his own.

He had provided well for his family, and it pleased him.

He finished his preening, yawned lazily, his gaping jaws noiseless, and then he was gone, merging into the background. It was time to take a well earned rest.

Chapter 17

For all is Vanity

In the cold farmhouse, a dim light shone through the kitchen window as the farmer prepared for his dawn visit to the flock. Lambing time was one of the busiest, most important periods of the year and the sheep had to be checked at first light and continually, throughout the day, until they settled down at dusk. Inevitably, the night brought more lambs to the flock for it is a mysterious fact that most of the births took place in darkness. By some strange pattern of nature, the ewes would face the new day with their new lambs beside them, steady and gaining in strength as they observed what was, for them, their first sunrise.

He knew immediately of the fox's visit.

He saw the ewe with her single lamb and saw the two afterbirths where she had lain.

He saw, further away, the bloodstains and the white wool, the pieces of bone and offal.

He followed the marks of the flattened grass to the gate, and he looked out into the distance, almost as if he hoped to see some trace of the invader. He quickly checked the rest of the flock and then, with all haste, he made off over the mountain in the direction of the huntsman's house.

There was no time to lose.

They must lay hounds to the scent before the heat of the day made detection impossible.

Last year, he had lost twenty-four lambs before the murderer, a small vixen with nine cubs to feed, had been traced. She had installed her brood in an earth, almost a mile away and had travelled far, to his fields, to kill, ignoring other lambs to do so.

Normally a killer fox would be found in close proximity but a traveller would be difficult to trace, leaving little scent as it retreated through the many lambing fields between the victim and the cubs.

Gareth, the huntsman, was seated at the breakfast table and the two friends ate together as the bad news was broken. They gulped the food, hastily, and when the meal was over, left to collect the hounds.

The big, strong, rough-coated Welsh hounds had already sung their song to the morning and it was their daily dawn chorus that regularly woke Gareth from his sleep. They crowded eagerly from their benches, noisily milling about at the railings and Gareth, pushing through the throng, began to choose his small pack for the day's work. He had no need to call to Dana and Traveller and Ranger. They were first through the gate and Gareth, choosing carefully, selected but a dozen of the most steady hounds in the kennels. He would not take a larger pack for, at lambing time, he did not wish to disturb the ewes any more than was necessary and so the small pack, and the two men, made their way over the mountain, to the scene of the evening's crime.

A few supporters were already there, alerted by messengers and, considering the short notice, it was a satisfactory gathering. When a fox began his assault on lambs, good support was certain, for nothing aroused more anger in the sheep farmers.

Scent was good.

The pack opened up their throats immediately, and the rousing cry carried away, far into the distance. It carried over the bracken and through the branches, it carried across streams and through hedges, it boomed over meadow and marsh and it seeped, faintly, under the cover of a heavy gorse patch, awakening, instantly, the russet form that lay curled at rest, with his brush over his muzzle.

Cadno knew instinctively, that the song was sung especially for him, and he was on his feet in an instant. The pack were over a mile away but, if his scent had been strong, they would soon be upon him.

He had not slept long, but he was refreshed.

He would soon confuse his pursuers.

He made off down the hillside until he gained the road and, once on the hard surface, he trotted for half a mile before leaving, where a small track led down to a narrow river. He crossed the river, climbed the opposite bank, and immediately dived back down, and into the water. Facing him in the garden of a cottage, he had seen two huge, dull-witted, slow-moving mastiff-type dogs and he had no wish to advertise his presence to such potential enemies.

He fled, running, splashing along the watercourse and returned to the opposite bank, half a mile downstream.

The hounds were in full cry and, as the followers struggled to stay with them, hopes were high that they would quickly find the breeding earth where the vixen would, perhaps, lay with her cubs. They surely would not have far to go.

When Cadno had left the rabbit at the earth, he had, by chance, retraced his footsteps for some distance and had slept contentedly in the gorse and so, when the hounds arrived at his sleeping place, they soon picked up the fresh scent and were off in pursuit towards the road.

The cubs were safe for the moment.

The pack lost vital moments on the hard surface, where the scent did not hold well, and they almost passed the spot where Cadno had headed for the river but, checking quickly, they crossed the water and climbed the bank, leaping into the garden and promptly facing the challenge of the two huge dogs. They lost ten minutes before Gareth managed to get them back on the line, downstream, and by now, he knew that they were not hunting a vixen. It was going to be a long, hard day.

Cadno was confident, his old arrogance came flooding to him.

The hounds had run the road, almost in silence, and the fox believed he had already beaten them. He had waited in a woodpile, branches and trunks and trash in a mighty heap, a favourite haunt for foxes and a safe resting place for many. He did not expect to hear them again that day but he soon paid the penalty for his over-confidence.

Sweeping into the field, the leading hounds were hunting at tremendous speed. The fox, from his hide, could see the hounds bearing down upon him and now, for the first time, he knew fear. Soon the woodpile was the object of attention for the dozen hounds and he sensed it to be only a matter of time before the men arrived. He cowered at the thought of this and moved, with caution, looking for a chance to bolt. The followers came into the field and Gareth, sizing up the situation immediately, blew three blasts on his hunting horn. The signal for the terriers.

The little devils would soon have him out.

Before the notes had echoed back from the woods, Cadno bolted from the tangle of logs and branches, like a red flash. He had chosen well in his bid for survival. Most of the hounds were on the opposite side of the pile, but nevertheless, the frantic cry was soon raised, and he ran for his very life.

He entered the woods barely a hundred yards ahead of the speedy Dana but, using all his crafts and calling upon all his instincts, he managed to open up a useful lead. He had run at his fastest and his flanks heaved and his tongue drooped from his mouth and his jaws hung wide as he gasped life-giving breath into his burning lungs. Into a clear field now, and on, past two stagnant pools and Cadno splashed through the still water, green, evil-smelling, undisturbed and covered with weed and slime and the fox, unhesitantly plunged in. He disappeared under the clinging surface only to climb out quickly and continue across the field toward the rabbit warren. The hounds, confused, lost him again.

When the huntsman arrived, he decided to try for a mark down at the warren. It appeared to be his only chance, perhaps they had pushed their fox hard enough for him to run to ground. But Cadno had not gone to ground. He was not yet done, and the dip in the water had revitalised him, but when the hounds failed to mark at the warren, the huntsman cast them about and, fortunately, as the effect of the stinking water faded, Dana once again reacted to the ancient curse of the fox. The fresh scent. The chase continued.

Cadno was well aware of the hounds. He knew he was still being hunted and he knew that the day would be difficult. The first signs of real tiredness appeared in his limbs and, once again, anxiety became his partner.

Tom Flanders had guessed at the line of flight and had crossed over the mountain, hoping that he was right. He stood, motionless, alongside some rocks, his two terriers at his side, his shovel secured to his back, and he scanned the countryside below. He saw the distant speck, moving steadily over the fields and knew it was the hunted fox even before the hounds came into sight. As it approached, he could plainly see its features and he also saw, and heard the pressing hounds, running hard, gaining rapidly.

Cadno sprang to the top of a dry-stone wall, approaching it sideways and hurling himself up with an agility that defied his exhausted condition. He ran along it for seventy yards and then dropped down on the other side. Suddenly, the fox, running along a narrow valley, checked, turned and climbed steadily up a steeply sloping field, towards a farm. Cadno ran through the farmyard where a sheepdog pranced at the end of a chain and then, quite deliberately it seemed, he plunged into the muck heap alongside the cowshed. His head and shoulders were visible as he struggled through to the opposite bank and then he made off, down the field, to resume his headlong flight along his original course. The deviation had cost him precious minutes. He was weary, and the hounds were very close. It was as if the fox had deliberately reasoned out his course of action, had chosen a method of confusing his relentless pursuers. Tom believed that they could not think as humans thought and did not believe them to be so cunning and scheming as they were credited with being and yet, at times such as this, he was faced with evidence which seemed to prove otherwise.

Tom had seen it all.

They had him now.

He had only to call the hounds to the line.

They would see the fox as he traversed the open moor, in full view for much of the time. The hounds had run well, they surely deserved their reward.

Tom leaned against the rock, undecided.

He stepped forward.

The hounds were following the line, up to the farm.

Let them.

If Cadno were the lamb killer, then he would have to die. But could they be certain? Perhaps some vixen had killed, not this fox that Tom had known and pursued for so long.

It was better to be sure.

He had promised himself that Cadno would one day face Bruiser, and the obsession was as great as ever. His old dreams of the battlefield were rare. They had been replaced with night visions of foxes and badgers and terriers, beast spirits from the infernal regions of an animal empire.

He saw hairless foxes with stinking, putrid flesh, dripping from their bones.

Piercing live eyes would look out and grinning, white-boned, diabolic skulls, frozen in gruesome posture, would zoom towards his face.

One night, he had seen Bruiser transformed into a hairy caterpillar and he had thrown it into the fire only to see it shrivel in the flames and turn back into the dwarf-like form of Bruiser, who had died howling at him in reproachful agony.

Soon, he had been pursued by badgers.

As fast as greyhounds.

He could not outrun them and he saw his body thrown into a nether world where it was consumed by a thousand grubs, all having the detailed appearance of tiny, wriggling badgers.

Kindness had been drummed into him.

As a child, he had cared for unfortunate animals, wild and domesticated. Sometimes when he awoke in his silent home, he would wonder if his mind was losing its way. His subconscious had managed to subdue and control his horror at the trench warfare but now he was plagued by new images, just as fiendish. He hoped that Jane, if she came to him, would disperse his nightmares with her soft, warm, comforting presence.

Cadno must not fall to the pack.

He belonged to Bruiser.

Tom watched the hounds follow through the farmyard.

He saw them flounder into the muck heap, saw them wrestle

their way, deeply, through the mire, which could hardly support their weight.

Watched as they struggled to free themselves from the clinging mess and remained silent as they cast about, in vain, to regain the line.

He said nothing when Gareth arrived and he helped him to gather the pack. They had covered about fourteen miles and the trek to the kennels would be a long and weary one.

Tom and Gareth coupled up the hounds for an immediate start to the homeward journey. The pack was tired, every hound had given his best and if they were allowed to relax now, to lie down, they would not be stirred for quite a time, no matter how their huntsman cajoled or threatened them. It was essential to keep them moving.

Though Cadno may have become a killer of lambs, Tom still admired him and could not grudge his his freedom. He thought again of the fox's actions to foil the pack. Was it mere chance which had taken him through a stinking pool, which he could have easily avoided? What had driven him to make the detour which took him across the rotting pile? No animal was able to think in such a manner. It must be, he thought, the vibrant power of genetic impulse, passed mysteriously along the generations. It must be conveyed in the everlasting spark of life that the parent passed on to the sibling.

He had never known such a fox.

Surely he was watched over by a greater presence.

Good luck to you Cadno, he thought, I don't suppose you will be back.

Two nights later, Cadno hunted the fields and carried another rabbit to his cubs.

* * * * *

A fox does not connect lamb-killing with the retribution of man.

He is cautious because he knows of man's presence and proximity.

To Cadno, lambs had been provided for his benefit, at a time when he was grateful for their availability. They were just

Carried a rabbit to his cubs.

another food source, easily killed, easily carried. The two-legged upright creatures were *always* his enemy for, truthfully could it be said that every man's hand was turned against the fox.

When fox families required their greatest nourishment, nature, albeit aided by man, provided it. Sometimes lambs were killed for no apparent reason and were left where they were slain, with the evidence of pin sharp teeth-marks at the throat. Sometimes the head and tail would be removed and more than once, a tail would be found alongside a vixen in a breeding earth. The carnage at lambing time varied from year to year but when particularly heavy losses occurred, farming lore and farming legend were added to, ensuring the fox to be ever looked upon as a villain, worthy of neither mercy nor respect.

The night was cold and a keen wind dried the pasture and the sheep were restless. In a corner of the field, marshy and unsuitable, a new life came painfully into the world as a gentle ewe strained with a difficult birth, and Cadno passed her without a glance. All life begins with pain of some sort and sometimes it is worthwhile and sometimes it is not.

Small lambs, sickly lambs, frail lambs, did not merit the fox's attention that night, though at another time they may have been his first choice. New born-lambs, heavily scented, helpless, coated with their birth fluids, were ignored. When the farmer came to the field before dawn, he would immediately see that his biggest, strongest, best lamb had vanished, leaving its mother standing near a crimson-coloured patch on the close-cropped grass. Cadno, true to the unpredictable manner of his tribe, deliberately selected his victim and killed without remorse. He ripped at the stomach cavity and washed his face in the warm blood and enjoyed the tender, tasty innards. When he was filled, he carried away the remainder, the body handing from his jaws and, struggling sometimes, hampered by the size and weight of his prize, he dragged it through hedges and over the stream and he pulled it along a sheep track and then, eventually gaining a well-balanced grip, he carried it for the last half mile, to the vixen's earth. He watched his growing family as they enjoyed the meat he had provided and then, silently, secretly, he withdrew, retracing his steps, as had become his habit, and snuggling down into a warm couch at a safe distance. He had fed well and was content. Content with his life and the progress of his family.

Soon it would be time to lead the litter to a new earth for they were rapidly outgrowing their present accommodation, but, now, he could rest, for surely, he had earned it.

* * * * *

An outraged farmer called out the hounds. His best lamb, a lovely ewe, healthy and strong. He had watched her, with pride, every day. She had been safe. No danger could threaten her, she was too big for a fox, nothing could despoil her. And now she was gone, while lesser animals wobbled about in weakness, and doomed-to-die ram lambs survived, in mocking splendour.

* * * * *

The chase was a short one, and hectic.

The hounds had flown along the fruity trail of Cadno's journey and, before he realised it, before he was thoroughly roused from his deep, well fed, contented sleep, they were upon him.

He could not avoid them.

He was in a stupor, heavy, cumbersome almost, and his distended stomach rumbled and the milling pack, howling were all about him.

He fell between two tussocks and scrambled through the maze of legs and somehow he was clear and running, with all the speed he could command.

Fear, nerve-stretching fear, gave added fleetness to his feet and he raced down the slope, his mind, his instincts, totally tuned to the twin tasks of his own survival and, despite his perilous position, the need to run away from the vicinity of the cubs and their mother.

Six hundred yards, every step taken in panic.

Six hundred yards in which certain death rode at his shoulder.

For one mad moment he was tempted to turn and go down defiantly, fighting in the face of his foes but he still could not yield to the inevitability of death.

He was out in the open, with no cover to hide him.

Forty yards ahead an earth in the bank beckoned him to its safety. He could hear the pounding feet close behind.

The fury in the screaming voices of the hounds told him of his extreme danger and he applied himself frantically to one last torrid effort to ensure his own survival.

He felt a great muzzle strike at him and hot breath swamped over him and he twisted and saw the lunging hound overbalance and then the darkness swallowed him and he hurtled into the haven of the cool, damp earth, voiding himself, in his fear, as he did so.

* * * * *

"Tom, bring Bruiser, it's the fox with the torn ear."

He had not needed to be told.

He would recognise Cadno among a thousand foxes, even without the all-revealing feature which disfigured his head.

The broad, flat head, the immense bulk, the unmistakable, arrogant attitude. he was quite the biggest fox that Tom had ever seen. Wolf-like, now that he had fully matured, he would dwarf Bruiser.

How would the little terrier cope with such a fearsome opponent?

The fox had dominated his thoughts on many a long night as he dozed by the fire.

He had prayed for its safety. He had willed it freedom from harm. He had wished it to travel paths of immunity, refuge and sanctuary. He knew that such an animal must die. The safety of the flocks, the good reputation of the pack, demanded it.

But let its last moments be lived out in the darkness of the earth.

Let him fall, if fall he must, to Bruiser.

He hauled himself slowly, and with some difficulty, up the steeply sloping banking, forcing his way through the closely planted pines and stooping low to avoid the whiplash effect of the branches. It required more effort than he remembered and his knee throbbed with a hot pain since he had twisted it awkwardly, earlier in the day. Still, he was eager with anticipation and could hardly wait to arrive at the bury where the hounds would be marking fiercely. He had not been near when Cadno had started his escape, for he had gone to a position lower down the valley, expecting, anticipating, the fox would run that way, but he had recognised Cadno immediately, even at some distance and saw that the big fox had not been able to choose his route for escape and now Tom, and Bruiser, would be the last to reach his refuge.

It was difficult to tell who was the most keen, Tom, or the little black terrier, straining at the lead, pulling relentlessly in the direction of the sound of the hunting horn.

* * * * *

There was a spring-fresh brightness to the day. The keen wind had long since died but the morning was still cool, though the blue sky was clear and clean with just a little hazy cloud. The fields were coming to a restful emerald green and the hedgerows showed signs of the abundant blossom which would soon clothe them. As Tom and Bruiser emerged onto the springy turf, he could not fail to be impressed by the beauty and the irony of it all. He had really expected the lamb killer to be a vixen with cubs and yet, here he was, on his way to enter Bruiser to Cadno.

Perhaps the fox had a vixen and brood in the area. If so, Tom hoped they would not be in the earth which Cadno had been forced to use and where he now waited.

He was on his way to end a life when, all about him, life was being created. As the animal kingdom ensured its continued survival, he was about to do all in his power to bring to an end the life of a creature he had once, so long ago it seemed, rescued from a miserable existence and released into the freedom which was its birthright.

* * * * *

For half an hour, Cadno had listened to the hounds as they ripped and tore at the earth, their frustration at his narrow escape giving them added determination. He had recovered from the fast, hair-raising chase and had composed himself as best he could. He had used this earth in the past and felt secure within its familiar confines. There were escape routes available for him if he needed to chance his luck by bolting but, for now, he squatted, wary, alert, but at rest. His breathing had slowed and returned to normal and a cool, fresh current of air revitalised him as it flowed through the tunnels. Soon it would cease.

Tom arrived at the bury and fastened Bruiser to a tree, using a chain, for the terrier, in his impatience to go to work, would very soon bite through a leather or rope restraint. The hounds had already sealed four of the entrances, trenching the earth so that it would be difficult to find the holes, but Tom checked all other possible escape routes and working quickly and methodically, sealed them all, except for one.

There was no way out now.

Cadno, below the ground, realised that the air flow had diminished and moved further into the bury and Tom, releasing Bruiser from his collar, rubbed his ears and carried him over to the one remaining, open entrance. He spoke softly to the writhing, struggling terrier, trying to clam him a little but, as he released him from his grasp, Bruiser disappeared into the tunnel with a headlong rush.

Cadno pushed under an overhanging stone, squeezing his bulk into a tight corner and, to his horror, realised there was no way to pass any further. Anxiously, he retraced his route but he knew he was trapped and in mortal danger.

He recognised the scent of a terrier and knew that soon he would need to defend himself.

He prepared to do so in the only way he knew.

Crouching, tense as a spring, with his jaws agape, he waited.

If he was to die, if this haven were to become his tomb, then he would sell his life for as great a price as he could secure. Yet, air had once more started to percolate through the passages. One hound, unseen, had reopened a blocked entrance and then moved away from it.

Was there to be, even now, a chance to cheat them once more, just once more?

* * * * *

The overwhelming scent of his enemy had met Bruiser full in the face. The space was confined, limited, and he had great difficulty in moving through the constricted passages. He had entered at a hole which was rarely used and he had to push and wriggle and force until his legs and chest were free. It was a flinty earth and his shoulders and flanks scraped through the unyielding tunnel but eventually, he reached the main passages and found more freedom of movement. Now he had only roots to contend with. Some where thin, weak things, easily snapped or pushed aside but two were as thick as a man's wrist and effectively cut the space in half, forcing the terrier to dig his way under them, removing enough earth to allow him to pass.

He was close to Cadno.

He knew it.

Could sense his presence.

Bruiser was, for the moment, trapped, half-way under the thick root, and he worked frantically to pull himself through.

As he did so Cadno charged.

The dog heard the low, rumbling sound of the growl in the back of the fox's throat and his sensitive ears honed in to the direction of the fox's approach. The strike was going to come from Bruiser's right side and he tried to turn his head to ward off the impending blow.

He was too late.

Bruiser could hardly move and the big fox struck at him again and again, driving his huge fangs deep into the terrier's muzzle. The black foreface became a mask of crimson gore and still the fox hammered home his advantage over the helpless terrier.

It would have been more than enough for many working terriers.

The sustained attack would have driven all but the best from the earth, but the punishment only served to rouse Bruiser to greater effort.

He knew he had to free himself.

With a last, enormous strain, he forced himself backwards and suddenly, he was free from the pressing captivity of the root and the punishing rapier-like teeth of the fox. As Cadno struck again, forcing his face past the root, Bruiser met him head on and gripped him loosely, hurriedly, at the cheek. It was the fox's turn to strain for release but the grip had been a hurried one, a defensive parry rather than an attack and, turning lithely, like a cat, Cadno freed himself and withdrew, perhaps realising at that moment that the oponent facing him in the darkness was the most deadly foe he had ever encountered.

He was faced with a stout-hearted animal that would not, could not, admit defeat.

An animal whose only purpose in life was to win.

An animal made sensible and brave by continued work and one who endured any hardship rather than give way to the adversary which now stood before him.

The fox quickly retreated, forcing himself under the overhanging, protruding stone, into the confined space behind it. Fresh air seemed to seep in, above his head and he tore at the earth with his teeth and scratched hard, at full stretch, with his feet.

Perhaps he could open a way through to another tunnel. Perhaps this would be his escape route, for there was no way for him to pass the terrier that stood his ground and never retreated, never gave an inch.

Turning, he faced the darkness from which his relentless pursuer would emerge. He waited, jaws open, to punish him once more.

He had not long to wait.

As Bruiser thrust his head into the recess, Cadno clamped his jaws over the terrier's muzzle. He held his grip, increasing the power and the pressure and the long fangs penetrated deep into Bruiser's face, slicing through his nostrils, piercing the soft flesh at the cheeks and ripping through to the gums. The terrier was unable to open his mouth and breathed with difficulty, labouring to draw air into his lungs, as Cadno maintained his advantage, waiting, expecting his opponent's body to collapse limply. Slowly, imperceptibly, the fox's muscles tired from the strain and gradually, the vice-like hold slackened until, with a sudden movement, Bruiser freed himself.

Inches from the fox, baying threateningly, non-stop, the terrier began to scrape away the earth, making room, more room, for a final assault. He knew he must have space to move with relative freedom. The instant he forced his head under the stone, he would be an easy target once more, unable to retaliate, completely vulnerable and methodically but with a controlled fury, he set himself the task of opening up the aperture, drawing the earth loose and flinging it behind him.

Three feet above him, he heard a spade strike the ground and knew that Tom had found him and was digging towards him. Cadno was also aware of the sound from the surface and renewed his attempts to dig through to an escape passage, taking advantage of his brief respite from Bruiser's attentions.

* * * * *

Closer now.

Tom was closer to Bruiser, Bruiser closer to Cadno.

The terrier, on his side, inched under the rock and Cadno, striking hard, tore teeth from the upper right jaw of the terrier. As he did so, Bruiser, ignoring the pain, indeed, not even feeling it, contorted himself and slammed his head into the underside of the fox's jaw. Clamping himself firmly, he kept his vital hold for a time and then he began to shift his grip, moving down, along the throat until soon, the life-giving oxygen passage to the lungs had been sealed.

Cadno, in his struggles, has dislodged a stone at the roof of his tomb and cool air rushed through to him. Mere inches above, a damp escape passage led straight to the entrance which the hound had opened.

Bruiser fought to maintain his final, deadly hold as Cadno, despairingly, struggled to free himself. Earth dribbled onto the terrier's tight-heaving body. He knew the diggers were directly above him. He meshed his jaws tightly together, the muscles of his neck and shoulders rigid.

Across the valley, deep in the cool, dark ground, a diminutive fox cub, lying apart from his sisters, stirred restlessly and yawned, his small, gaping jaws open wide, and the circle of life continued.

For they have all, but one breath, and man is just another animal.

For all life is vanity and, with certainty, all return to the dust.